SONNY (BURT REYNOLDS) FACED

"THE END"

with a little help from his friends:

Marlon Borunki *(Dom DeLuise)*—Sonny's buddy in the nuthouse; ingenious, frustrated, and criminally insane.

Mary Ellen *(Sally Field)*—the girl friend; cute as a button but missing a few marbles.

Jessica *(Joanne Woodward)*—the ex-wife; pre-occupied with her broken washing machine and mustachioed Latin lover.

Marty *(David Steinberg)*—his lawyer friend; it takes more than a shyster lawyer to talk Sonny out of suicide.

Dad *(Pat O'Brien)*—paints by the numbers and causes *Mom (Myrna Loy)* to pop pills—where else would Sonny get the stuff that permanent dreams are made of. . . .

"THE END"

A Novel by
CAROL STURM SMITH
Based on the Screenplay by
JERRY BELSON

AVON
PUBLISHERS OF BARD, CAMELOT AND DISCUS BOOKS

THE END is an original publication of Avon Books.
This work has never before appeared in book form.

AVON BOOKS
A division of
The Hearst Corporation
959 Eighth Avenue
New York, New York 10019

Copyright © 1978 by Avon Books and Wendell Films, Inc.
Published by arrangement with Wendell Films, Inc.
Library of Congress Catalog Card Number: 78-53128
ISBN: 0-380-01978-7

First Avon Printing, May, 1978

AVON TRADEMARK REG. U.S. PAT. OFF. AND IN
OTHER COUNTRIES, MARCA REGISTRADA,
HECHO EN U.S.A.

Printed in Canada

PART ONE

Prologue

SAUL KRUGMAN, M.D., F.A.C.S., F.R.C.S. (Hon.), hematologist, put aside the twelve folders his nurse had left in his in-box and went to the window of his office on the eighth floor of the Medical Building. It was going to be a bad morning. He had three patients with less than a year to live to see before noon. He looked down at the parking lot, at the human traffic leaving and entering cars, walking the paths to the entrances. It was a beautiful day in the Santa Barbara hills; the blue of the sky was magnificent.

Dr. Krugman glanced at his watch and wondered if his nurse guessed at this morning ritual, the standing at the window waiting until someone inevitably sighted the plaque on the wall near the main entrance's revolving door. THE MEDICAL BUILDING: A PROFESSIONAL CORPORATION, it said. Sometimes the sign was sighted in just a few minutes; rarely did it take the full thirty minutes he allowed himself to window-gaze and think after scanning the folders on office-visit mornings. He used the time to organize his thoughts, to anticipate the questions and prepare answers. It helped enormously. For the most part, the people who came to him wanted reassurance, information about pain, and. . . .

A man in his early sixties with an East Coast suit habit, driving a black Hertz Ford, was opening the passenger door for a lovely woman in her early twenties, blonde, petite, well-dressed, high color in her cheeks. Daughter or mistress? Saul wondered. Daughter, probably. The gentleman was handling her arm like a father. He's the one, Saul thought suddenly, glancing at his watch. Only seven minutes this morning. And sure enough, the man stopped at the main door for a moment, gave a quick wave in the direction of the sign, and snorted a laugh that Saul could almost hear, the way he could almost hear the birds chirping in the clear morning air outside his window. Then the man was talking gently to his beautiful blonde daughter, explaining why he had laughed, no doubt, a learned smile on his face, and they disappeared through the revolving door leading to the Medical Building's main reception area on the ground floor.

Saul returned to his desk, tapped the files into a neat pile, and put them in the basket to the right of the telephone. When he had first noticed the amount of attention the sign on the entrance wall received, several months after he had taken the office, he could not understand it. But over the years he realized that the people accompanying those who came as patients to the medical center used the sign to attempt a change of mood away from dread. Wealthy people came here for consultation, people with good health insurance, people to whom the idea of medicine as a corporate entity would provoke reactions. He often wondered at the content of the comments; were they as predictable as the content of the dialogue he had with his patients? He wondered if the young blonde woman was even now in the elevator heading for the eighth floor and his office. She fit the description in one of his folders.

"What you have is the same thing Ali MacGraw had in *Love Story*," he would have to say to her, and suddenly Saul wished that he were somewhere else, anywhere else.

The buzzer on his intercom sounded three short dots, the signal from his nurse that his first three patients had arrived. Some days they were all late, but, often as not, they would come early. He took ice from the small refrigerator in the bathroom for the thermos pitcher, filled it with water, and placed the carafe on the tray on the table beneath the wall mirror. He replenished the supply of paper cups. He adjusted the blinds. He liked these small tasks; they helped him enter a mood which he found necessary to be effective.

He took one last look around the office, moved the leather chair across from his desk a fraction of an inch, and only then returned to his chair and reached for the first folder. He placed it squarely on the desk before him, opened it with no further preliminaries, and began a quick review.

Wendell Sonny Lawson. Called Sonny, no doubt, Saul thought, or he wouldn't give his middle name. Thirty-nine. Divorced. One child, a daughter. Parents both alive; mother sixty, father seventy. No serious illnesses as an adult. Measles, mumps, and chicken pox. Appendix removed at age fourteen. The mother had hypertension. No family history of diabetes, cancer, heart disease. Reports from other physicians. The results of a biopsy, a spinal tap, and very recent blood tests. Saul looked at the recent test results.

"No, you do not have the same thing Ali MacGraw had in *Love Story*, Mr. Lawson," Saul would say. "That was leukemia. You have a toxic blood disease."

"Yes, but I wind up the same way, don't I? Dead?"

"I didn't say that."

"You didn't say it because"—Saul looked at the written reports in the front of the file; Mr. Lawson had consulted three other doctors—"because you guys can't keep making a living by referring me to each other if you tell me I'm almost dead. Now, how much longer have I got?"

Saul put away the blood test results and began evaluating the results of the spinal tap and biopsy.

"That's hard to say."

"Try."

"There's always a chance that some doctor working

9

in a lab somewhere will. . . ." Saul looked through all the lab reports quickly one more time. It really was not good.

"A year. Eighteen months at best." It was better to be honest. Kinder, in the long run.

He turned to the front of the file and began reading the most recent physician's report. Mr. Lawson was in a period of remission. He had taken off considerable weight in the last few months. People frequently took on an almost glowing quality when they were in remission. If he was a good-looking man, even slightly vain, Mr. Lawson would probably get up at this point and look in the mirror, using the water pitcher on the table as an excuse. He would take his time, pour and drink, and look in the mirror.

"What's the worst?" he would say after a moment.

"Well . . . I've seen some cases with patterns such as yours go in three months, but I would expect you to have a year."

Saul wondered if Mr. Lawson would curse. He referred quickly to the front of the folder. Probably. He was a Catholic. He'd say, "Jesus. Jesus Christ. I knew I was sick, but how come I don't feel like I'm dying? I feel lousy, but not like I'm dying. I thought it was good that I was losing weight. Everyone had been telling me how great I look. Look at me, Dr. Krugman. I look great. Don't I look great?"

"I wish you'd seen your own doctor sooner." Saul never could restrain himself from this one mild censure of the people who came to consult him when it was already too late for real help; it seemed like such a waste. "Surely you must have started feeling ill quite some time ago."

"I thought I'd discovered a new diet—throwing up," someone had said just a few mornings before. The remark had forced Saul's face into a wry smile.

He wondered if Mr. Lawson had a sense of humor. It was possible. He was experiencing pains in his stomach—probably about a six-level on a scale of ten—but was not having headaches. Unconsciously Saul began making treatment plans. For a moment, while reading the second of the three accompanying reports, Saul had a passing fancy that a spleen removal might help. But it wouldn't, he knew. There was no sense in subjecting Mr. Lawson to unnecessary procedures. Drugs to combat the pain, of course. Bone marrow injections. Chemotherapy . . .

"Tell me exactly what it will feel like . . . toward the very end." Saul had a hunch that Mr. Lawson would want to know. He was well educated, made a good living. Saul always answered this question straight.

"During the final stages, you'll have to be hospitalized. You'll have shortage of breath, severe cramps, and rectal hemorrhaging."

Saul Krugman sighed and checked Mr. Lawson's medical insurance record. Good, he thought. It was adequate. Because Mr. Lawson would ask the inevitable.

"Will I have control over my bowels?"

"No," Saul would say. And then, in a worthwhile attempt at a laugh, he would add, "But at least I can promise you one thing."

"What?"

"A private room."

Chapter One

THIS IS ALL WRONG, Sonny Lawson thought suddenly. It's all wrong. His sinuses and throat and the back of his eyes were tight with unshed tears. He felt as he had felt leaving summer camp as a boy, but then the phenomenon had been of a sense of things speeding up —of the trip home taking no time at all while it had taken forever to get there in the first place. And what had happened to the sound track that should be accompanying this, the first day of the last three months of his life? Three months, Dr. Krugman had said. Three months! He could hear his own footsteps on the lobby floor, but no sounds at all from anyone else. He was walking in a vacuum, a bubble. Descending in the elevator, Sonny had not been able to suppress one single anguished moan, one single pounding of his doubled fists against the back wall, an action that the elevator had taken as a cue to stop and silently open itself onto a corridor; and silently the other passengers had filed out, eyes unanimously facing front, leaving Sonny alone. The button he had pushed to bring him to the lobby hadn't even clicked, he remembered, and a strange ringing, like muted church bells, had filled the space vacated by the people. The redheaded receptionist with the voice like a frog still manned the information desk—on his way up to Dr. Krugman's office Sonny had stopped there for directions, and her voice had stayed with him, odd patches of words cutting through the foyer to reach him even while he had stood and waited at the elevator bank at the far end. Now the nurse was moving her mouth at a plump woman in a plaid dress, but Sonny could hear only the dull *click click* of the rubber heel protectors on his shoes.

And then finally he attained the revolving door and was out in the sunshine, and the sound of other feet on gravel and the noise of traffic and a shrill high laugh from a girl child and the voices of the birds assaulted him. He reached out at an imaginary wall to steady himself as a pain hit him in the stomach. At least a six, maybe a seven. A thin line of sweat beaded up beneath his moustache, and when he reached a hand to his face he realized that he was crying, but the pressure in his head, behind the eyes, had not eased.

"Why me? Oh, God, why me?" The unexpected sound of his own voice shocked Sonny into an awareness of himself and his surroundings. He hadn't meant to speak the words aloud. The pain in his stomach retreated. He looked around guiltily to see if his actions had been noticed. Then, ignoring the KEEP OFF signs, he headed for the fountain in the middle of the landscaped circular area surrounded by the parking lots.

The water felt cool and delicious.

He washed his face and dried himself with his handkerchief and watched the passage of a little girl and her mother. The woman, a drawn look on her pretty face, had the child tight by the hand. The little girl—was she the little girl whose laugh he had heard earlier?—was wearing a blue dress with a ruffled skirt. She reminded Sonny of his daughter, Julie. Julie had worn a dress with ruffles for a birthday party, what, six years ago? Seven? Oh, Lord, how was he going to tell Julie? The woman and child were heading for the revolving door leading to the medical center's lobby. Sonny turned and watched the woman's buttocks play beneath her tight, well-fitting pants. Nice, he thought. Nice. And then, with a shrug, he headed for the Jaguar. Why him? Why not him?

And he had a sudden yen for smog, for grayness, for acrid smells, for mist, rain, anything but the beauty of this Santa Barbara day. To have to face the certainty of his death on a day such as this was an irony so massive that he could not quite fathom it. It was going to give him indigestion. He was going to have to be careful not to overfeed his self-pity. Sonny glanced at his watch. Maybe he could track Marty down at lunchtime. No time like the present to check out his will and insurance policies. Maybe he'd have Marty sell the Jaguar and pass the money along to Mary Ellen. If he left her anything in the formal will, then Julie and his parents. . . . Oh, Lord, how was he going to tell his parents?

He emitted a short, harsh laugh.

No sense in giving up a good parking place.

There was a parking ticket on the Jaguar's windshield.

With a sudden sense of purpose Sonny headed back to the medical center, taking the path marked HOSPITAL ENTRANCE.

It was as if the revolving door had taken him into an episode of "Twilight Zone." To his left was a reception desk, just as in the clinic building, but the redheaded nurse had become a dark-haired woman with a long neck. She reminded Sonny of a giraffe. The orderlies here were black, and the people all seemed to know where they were going—doctors out in plain sight, not hiding themselves behind office doors, and people who were patients and knew they were patients and were dressed like patients—and someone had stolen all the color. No men in patterned sports shirts or women with pink blouses. White everywhere, on all the people, and in the air was an all-pervading substance that swallowed the atmosphere itself and transformed it into an aroma that, Sonny realized suddenly, was the same everywhere on earth. He could be anywhere—Rangoon, or Buenos

14

Aires, or Toronto, or London. . . . He stopped an orderly who was pushing a cart of food trays.

"Where are the patients who are dying?"

"Everywhere," the orderly said.

"No," Sonny said, rejecting the statement, "I mean, one special place."

"I dunno, man. I ain't no doctor. I'm a singer. I just work here part-time."

"Come on, man," Sonny said, reaching out to grab the orderly's arm, half expecting him to break into a soft-shoe dance, "I gotta know. I'm dying. I've just got a couple of months to live."

The orderly reacted instinctively, yanking back and moving his cart. "Don't touch the food!"

"I'm sorry, I. . . ."

"Look," the orderly said, "try the third floor. None of those folks up there look like they're leaving this place. Least, not out the front door."

"Thanks," Sonny said, and he automatically headed for the back of the lobby, knowing that the elevators would be there. It was as if he had made this trip before, as if he belonged here in this place.

The air in the elevator seemed thick. There was a strange, hackle-raising quiet. Then the door slithered open and Sonny was on the third floor.

Gingerly he began walking down the hall, his mind rejecting what he was seeing, rejecting the image of himself parked in a wheelchair outside a room, plugged into portable tube-and-wire apparatuses.

He was heading quite blindly for the nurses' cubicle, which was halfway down the corridor, and he was startled by the unexpected appearance of a healthy-looking female dressed in white who appeared from behind a partition and watched him walk the last twenty feet. She must have heard his steps, Sonny realized.

"Can I help you?" the nurse asked.

"Uh, let's see," Sonny said. Why was he here? For a preview?

"Are you here to see one of the patients?" the nurse asked, cocking her head to the side and taking on an owlish expression.

"Yes, that's it," Sonny said quickly, fighting an impulse to feel his head to see if his own physiognomy had changed, was changing. "I'm here to see one of the patients."

"Which one?"

"The sickest one," Sonny said.

"Oh, Mr. Welch," the nurse said. "Thank God he's finally got a visitor. Are you a member of the family?"

"Oh, yes," Sonny said hastily, as an orderly stuck his head out of the cubicle to monitor the conversation. "I'm his nephew. We're very close. Where is he?"

"Six C," the nurse said, pointing down the hall.

"Thank you," Sonny said, and headed for what turned out to be the last room on the left-hand side of the corridor. The door was half-open, and Sonny entered without knocking.

It was a private room, with the shades drawn, dominated by the hospital bed in the center of the room and the complicated life-support machines that stretched tentacles to the bed from both sides. A dresser was in the room, and two chairs, and a large television set mounted on a support near the foot of the bed. All this Sonny saw before he could bring himself to look at the frightening apparition that occupied the bed, covered by a white sheet.

"Hi, Doc," the man said in a thin voice when Sonny finally met his eyes.

"Uh . . . hi," Sonny said. The man was old. So old. And his face and hands were not human-colored, but the color of pastry dough. No, he was yellow, like old paper. He had a tube in his nose, tubes in his arms, and wrinkles worked so deep into his face that his attempt at a smile sent grooves outward from his mouth like a stone sending ripples across a pond.

16

"Uh, how are you feeling?" Sonny asked before the pause in the conversation got too long.

"Yesterday was shitty," the old man said, his voice weak but friendly. "Today's been better. It's up to lousy."

Sonny moved closer to the bed. "Did you pass the night without too much pain?" he asked.

"You're not a doctor, are you?" the old man said then.

"No," Sonny confessed.

"I knew it!" the old man said. "You were only doing one thing at once."

"What?"

"A real doctor always does at least *two* things at once," the old man explained. "They ask you how you are while they poke you somewhere. Or they take your temperature while they check your chart. Always two things."

"You're right," Sonny said. "I'm not a doctor. The truth is . . . um . . . my wife . . . yes, my wife is very sick. She may have to come to a place like this. I . . . I just wanted to see . . ."

". . . how bad it was," the old man said, finishing Sonny's sentence.

"Yes," Sonny admitted. "I'm sorry. It was rude of me to just burst in here."

The old man shrugged, which seemed to cost him an effort. "Nobody knocks around here," he said. "The doors are always open."

That's just as bad as doors that are always locked, Sonny thought, just a different kind of jail, a different way of being unable to protect one's time and privacy. Anyone could walk in at any time, do anything, and when you're flat on your back in bed connected to machines, there isn't much you can do. What did the machines do, anyway? One was obviously feeding the old man, and another was obviously monitoring something vital, but it was still mysterious, as mysterious as the pipes and flaming exhausts on the oil refineries he had seen in New Jersey and Louisiana.

But now the old man was looking at him expectantly, as if the simple presence of a person in his room who wasn't a doctor was in itself yet another kind of artificially induced alteration of reality, as if he expected something, the same way he must have expected something when he allowed himself to be imprisoned in this open-door place where you were attached to machines.

And then Sonny realized that all the old man expected was that he explain himself further, or ask the questions he wanted to ask, and to get on with it.

"Would you like to tell me about your illness?" Sonny said.

"I don't mind," the old man said, shrugging, "but I swear to God it keeps changing. Every time I get a new pain, they come up with a new name for it. No new cures, mind you, just new names."

"I'm sure the doctors will—"

The old man shook his head and interrupted Sonny. "No, no, young man, don't bother trying to comfort me. The doctors have tried everything. I'm not going to live long enough to let them try anything more."

Sonny shuddered as a cough racked the old man's body, interrupting his speech. The noise hacked through the air and shook the old man's body; the tubes did not move, and Sonny realized they were taped securely in place.

"Thank God, it's almost over," the old man whispered as the cough ended. He lay back—the cough had stiffened his upper torso, making him rise slightly from the sheets, like an apparition pulled by strings—and groaned in pain.

"Can I do anything for you?" Sonny asked. "Call a nurse?"

The old man shook his head, his eyes closed now. A hint of perspiration appeared on his forehead then, delayed and meager, as if his body's sweating mechanism were a sprinkler system malfunctioning. The old man carefully wiped the moisture into his thin hair; he seemed to withdraw from the feel of his own skin.

"Jesus," Sonny said, frustrated and almost angry. "Don't you ever feel like just ripping off all this stuff? All these tubes and things?"

"Every day," the old man said. "But I haven't got the guts—or the strength."

"You could ask a friend."

"No," the old man said. He used his legs to hike himself slightly higher on the bed, as if to find comfort which he knew wasn't coming. "I wouldn't want to saddle anybody with the knowledge that they had caused my death."

"How about your wife?"

"I wouldn't give her the satisfaction," the old man said, a look of determination crossing his face. Sonny waited a bit, thinking that the old man was going to continue, but he didn't—instead, turned his face into the pillow, obviously very tired. Sonny knew he should leave, that he wasn't doing the old man any good—and what was he doing here, anyway?

"Look, I know I'm tiring you, but there's one other thing I'd like to ask. I hope it's not too personal."

"After four months of having a nurse change your diapers, nothing is too personal," the old man said.

"Well, I just wondered what it's like."

"What what's like?"

"Uh . . . what you're doing now," Sonny said lamely.

"You mean dying?" the old man asked.

Sonny nodded, unable to quite bring himself to say the word, grateful that the old man was making it easy for him.

"Well," the old man said, "I could bullshit you, but I guess you didn't come up here for bullshit, so let me tell you, dying stinks! It hurts, it's embarrassing, and it's expensive. It's not a good thing. They get you in the hospital and stick a tube in every hole God gave you. After that, they start making their own holes!"

The speech had cost the old man, and Sonny waited until a coughing spasm cleared and he once again opened his eyes.

"But what about day to day . . . hour to hour?" he asked. "I mean, is *that* any different from one day to the next?"

"Hmmmmm," the old man said, looking away from Sonny for a minute to think. "Well," he said at last, "a lot depends upon what's on TV." Then he wheezed a dry breath through his mouth and clutched at his chest and waved his hand into the air to indicate that he was exhausted, that he didn't want to talk anymore, and slowly Sonny backed out of the room and retraced his steps past the nurses' cubicle to the elevator.

The elevator stopped at the second floor, and a man in his twenties, pushing his own portable IV unit, entered.

"Got an important call to make," the young man said, winking at Sonny. "The phone's tied up here on two." The sight of the patient, up and moving around, was positively comforting to Sonny after the exposure he had just had to the wreckage on the third floor.

"I've got a call to make, too," Sonny said impulsively, suddenly needing to see Marty, desperately needing to see Marty, knowing suddenly that he was not going to allow himself to be bedded and tubed like the old man upstairs whose image was seared into his brain.

But it turned out that there was just a single phone in the alcove to the left and down a small corridor from the information booth on the main floor of the medical center's hospital building, and the young man with the IV unit—Sonny watched, annoyed but slightly amused as the young man carefully increased the flow of the glucose solution that was dripping into his arm from the transparent bottle on the unit just before he dropped his dime into the slot—made it to the phone first. The young man was clutching the receiver with both hands, tense, and then he relaxed and began talking, hunching into the plastic hood and speaking softly, turning once to smile at Sonny.

Marty Lieberman, Sonny's lawyer, had his office about a twenty-minute drive from the medical center. He was Sonny's oldest and best friend. They did business together; they had cheated on their wives together; they had both tried, unsuccessfully, to make it with Darleen Anderson, Marty's secretary, a wonderfully efficient woman who was in her late twenties now and had come to work for Marty straight out of high school.

"Naw, I feel fine," the young man was saying into the phone. "They're feeding me intravenously just to build up my strength, and I'm gonna need my strength for Saturday night, right, baby?"

The patient winked at Sonny, and then turned back to the phone. "Give me a kiss," he said into the receiver.

Impatient, Sonny reached out and turned the valve on the young man's IV unit, and in a matter of minutes, professing tiredness, the patient cut his hustle short. Sonny turned the man's IV unit back on as he shuffled past, and then he was dialing Marty's number.

"Law office," Darleen answered.

"Darleen, where's Marty? I need him."

"He just left, Sonny. He had a few errands to do and then he's got a lunch date with a client."

"Where's he lunching?"

"Why?"

"Why? Because I need to see him, that's why."

"Can't it wait? He's got a cozy little luncheon planned with a hot young divorce prospect, and I don't think he—"

"I don't care if he's lunching with. . . . Look, this is serious."

"Sure, Sonny."

"I mean it, Darleen. I've just come from the doctor, and I'm dying. I have no time."

"Are you serious?" Darleen's voice said she suspected it was a lie.

"You're damned right I'm serious."

There was a short silence on the other end of the phone, then Darleen said, "Casa Vega. The Mexican place. He'll kill me if you're putting me on, Sonny."

"Casa Vega. Thanks."

"He won't be there until one."

"Thanks. I'll see you . . . and then again, maybe I won't. 'Bye."

It was 11:35 A.M. when Sonny Lawson threw the gearshift into reverse, backed the Jaguar out of its parking place, and headed around the circular drive that led to the Medical Building complex exit. The parking ticket that had been on the windshield had been torn into small pieces and left behind on the ground. The pain in Sonny's stomach had begun again, and he was on the verge of nausea, grappling with dark thoughts and unknown feelings. There was too much to do, too many things to think about. He needed sanctuary, and did not know where to go. He had time to kill before seeing Marty. The Jaguar was filthy; perhaps he'd get it washed. He loosened a button on his sports shirt. It was hot. Very hot. He braked to a stop and let a black Ford pull out of a parking slot. The young blonde woman and her father who had been waiting in Dr. Krugman's office were in the car. The sight of them made him slightly dizzy—his time sense was distorted. The woman's face was pale; the man behind the wheel waved his thanks at Sonny. There was a sadness in the man's eyes so terrible that Sonny felt a pang, a physical kinship with the other's pain. It angered him. The Ford preceded him slowly, but was prevented from attaining the street by a uniformed guard, an employee of the medical center, a gray-haired man in a blue uniform with a ruddy face and pursed cheeks. The guard had stopped traffic from leaving the parking lot to allow a funeral cortege by on the hillside road. Two policemen on motorcycles had already passed, followed by a hearse and now what seemed like an endless procession of limousines. They were driving leisurely. To Sonny it seemed appropriate, just another of the day's little ironies, and yet, still haunted by the vision he had seen in the eyes of the man driving the car in front of him, Sonny could not control a sudden spurt of adrenalin, an unpremeditated urge that pushed his foot against the Jaguar's accelerator pedal, and turned his arms so the Jaguar pulled around the Ford, and deafened his ears to the frantic whistle of the guard.

Sonny headed the Jaguar into the oncoming traffic, driving parallel to the funeral cortege.

He was vaguely aware of startled faces in the limousines he passed—four, five, six, seven—who was this dude who'd died despite the weather which cried out for life?—and of the two teen-aged children and puffy-faced, crying widow in the first limousine, and then he pulled alongside and slowed to the speed of the hearse. He leaned over and rolled down his passenger side window.

"What did he die of?" Sonny yelled.

The hearse driver, a tough-looking character with a pockmarked face and thin hair combed forward over a high forehead, turned tentatively in Sonny's direction.

"What?" he yelled back. "What do you want?"

"The guy in back. What did he die of?"

"Whatta you, crazy?" the hearse driver yelled, his attention split between Sonny and the road. "Go away!"

"I just want to know what he died of," Sonny yelled back.

"I don't know what he died of. But I know what you're gonna die of!" The hearse driver shook his head in the direction of an oncoming cement truck, which was followed by an impatient BMW. Sonny jammed on the Jaguar's brakes and swerved behind the hearse. In

23

his rearview mirror he watched the uniformed driver of the limousine he had cut off fight and manage to control his vehicle. There was a flurry of black activity in the back seat of the limousine that for no apparent reason reminded Sonny of a cat fight.

He was sweating badly.

He was feeling and acting crazy.

He knew he was feeling and acting crazy, and he knew he had to apologize even if he could not control himself.

When the road in front of the cortege cleared, Sonny pulled the Jaguar back out of the lane and slowed to even up with the limousine, but before he could explain himself the limousine driver rolled down his window.

"You crazy bastard!" the driver spat at him. "I've got the family of the deceased here. Have a little respect!"

"I'm sorry," Sonny said. "I've just come to apologize." He nodded his head and waved at the mourners in the back seat. "I'm sorry. I'm dying, too, and I just wanted to know what he died of."

"Get him out of here, will you, officer?" the hearse driver said suddenly, and Sonny realized that one of the two policemen leading the cortege had dropped back from the front of the procession and pulled alongside the Jaguar.

"Get out of here," the policeman said to Sonny.

"I've got as much right here as anybody else," Sonny said, "except him." He pointed to the coffin in the back of the hearse. "Oh, God, and maybe *him*," Sonny yelled, and performed an intricate maneuver that successfully allowed him to outflank the policeman and avoid colliding with the yellow Camaro that had appeared from nowhere, driving too fast, heading straight for him. The Camaro rammed up on the sidewalk, screeching its brakes. The sound shivered in the air.

Two of the limousines went *scrunch;* the motorcycle policeman's siren entered the fray.

"All right, pull over!" the policeman screamed, color flushing his face. He pointed to a dirt turnoff that abutted the Santa Barbara Mission, a few yards ahead on Sonny's left. "I want you right there," the policeman said, "where I can see you. We are going to have a talk in three minutes!" He gunned his motorcycle and pulled back to the tangled limousines, no doubt to check for injuries.

Sonny dismissed a fleeting impulse to make a bootleg turn and escape in the Jaguar, watching the needles on the instrument panel climb, feeling the machine hug the road, taking the corners and hills as he had the first few weeks after he had bought the car. If the Camaro had not been blocking the road, he might have given it a try. What did he have to lose? Instead, he meekly pulled the Jaguar into the dirt turnoff and killed the engine. He was surprised that his escapade had taken him to Los Olivos Street and the Santa Barbara Mission; he could barely remember leaving Dr. Krugman's office. Three months, Dr. Krugman had said. He had always meant to go into the Mission; it was a magnificent church, a blending of old Spanish and Moorish architecture, of native sandstone, painted ivory. How long was it since he had been in church? Fifteen years? Twenty years? How does one spend three months when there isn't another three months after that to spend? He got out of the Jaguar to stretch and wipe his face and neck with his damp handkerchief. He held his hands out straight before him. They were steady. The pain in his stomach was gone. Its absence was a reminder that it would come again. Sonny knew with a sudden clarity that he would use his need to urinate as an excuse to go into the Mission.

Now the motorcycle policeman pulled into the turnoff, his foot scraping a small furrow in the dirt as he stopped and secured his bike. He was a big man, top-ping Sonny's six feet by at least two inches, and he carried his authority in the set of his straight backbone as well as in the gun in his holster and his badge and uniform and the inevitable ticket book he held in his left hand, flipping it open and producing a pen even as he walked the few paces that separated him from Sonny.

"Look, I had a very good reason for doing what I did," Sonny said, although in fact he could barely remember what had prompted him to pull his outrageous stunt.

"I'm sure you did," the policeman said. His voice was deep and held resignation. "And I've got a very good reason for giving you this ticket." But the policeman hesitated then, watching Sonny closely. Recognition had begun to flare in his eyes.

"Have I seen you somewhere before? I've seen you somewhere before, buddy," the policeman said.

"No, you've never seen me before," Sonny said.

"Yes, I have," the policeman said. "Somewhere up north, maybe. In a mug book?"

He must have seen the television spots for Lake Crest Estates, Sonny realized; but the memory didn't come to the man, and he turned his attention away from Sonny's face and began to write the license number of the Jaguar on a ticket.

"Here, let me save you some trouble." Sonny watched himself reach out and take the ticket book from the policeman, and carefully separate the ticket from the others. "Tickets mean nothing to a man in my condition," he heard himself say. He handed the ticket book back to the policeman and calmly tore the ticket into pieces.

"Drunken driving," the policeman said. "And littering." Anger at Sonny's strange behavior had begun to alter the policeman's expression.

"I'm going to tear it up."

"No, you're not."

"Yes, I am," Sonny said, a strange feeling of pleasure

26

prompting him. He wasn't afraid of this man. He wasn't worried about the ticket. He wasn't even worried about Lake Crest Estates. He wouldn't be around to face the hassle. The bells of the Mission had begun to chime the noon hour, and on the street cars were beginning to honk their frustration at the traffic snarl caused by the disrupted funeral procession. The hearse driver had left his vehicle to help the two limousines, which had locked bumpers, and the widow had left her limousine and was gesticulating wildly at the driver of the yellow Camaro, as if explaining that the man in the coffin was going to be late for an important lunch date.

Now the policeman waved at his partner, who had blown his whistle and indicated with a hand sign that he needed help, and with a gesture of frustration he wrote Sonny's license number in his book, slammed the cover closed with an audible sound, and replaced his pen in his shirt pocket.

"You haven't seen the last of me, buddy," the cop said, climbing back on his motorcycle and activating the starter. "My name is Brian Flannery, Officer Brian Flannery—that's Flannery with two *n*'s—and once I get this guy in the ground, I'm going to check you out with Motor Vehicles and get your address, and then I'm coming for you."

"Better hurry," Sonny said, turning his back on Officer Brian Flannery and heading across the dirt path toward the front door of the Santa Barbara Mission.

Sonny had driven past the beautiful old Spanish Mission, the Queen of Missions, hundreds of times. It was both a tourist attraction and a working church, but he knew that he would never have set foot on the grounds of the sanctuary if chance had not directed him here. But wasn't chance part of what it was all about, anyway?

With a sense of purpose he crossed the small bed of landscaping that separated the dirt turnoff from the vast front lawn of the church, walking between the Mission

27

house with its red-tile roof and the huge fountain on the lawn, heading for the church proper with its massive square front towers which were arcaded with domed belfries. He stood for a moment and looked at the design of the classic facade, snatches of a college lecture on architecture popping into his head: engaged columns of Ionic order, dentiled cornice, a frieze adorned with a heavy fret motif, a crowning pediment. In the tympanum of the pediment was a niched figure of Saint Barbara, and surmounting the pediment were three seated figures and a stepped gable cresting topped with a cross.

To his left was a door, which he suspected led to the Mission House and the left tower.

The door was locked.

Had people come here and climbed the spiral staircase in the tower and jumped?

The thought got him walking to the double paneled doors in the deeply recessed arched front entrance of the church. One of the doors was open. The vestibule was cool and beautiful and quiet with the quiet of peacefulness.

Sonny found his way to the rest room, and was startled when the sound of the toilet flushing reminded him of a sense of finality he had felt once—how old was he then? ten? eleven?—when leaving the safety of the bathroom before heading to confess the sin of masturbation to Father Conklin. He seemed to be flashing on long-buried episodes from his past with unusual frequency; there was an edge to his sense of reality; he felt both purposeful and directionless.

The interior of the Mission's long, narrow nave was lighted by small splayed windows in the side walls, and had a flat wooden ceiling, embellished with painted and carved rosettes. The walls were flanked by side altars with religious paintings above. In the first bay, left and right, were chapels, recessed in the deep side walls.

Sonny stopped and made a full circle in the aisle to take a better look, glad that the church was beautiful,

28

that it held its space reverently, as befits a place of worship, but he was surprised at the emptiness. He had expected the church to show signs of activity. He wondered where the priests were, why no one else had come to seek sanctuary here today.

Then he headed down the aisle toward the main altar, which was decorated with painted floral festoons and figures. He had spotted a teenaged boy with bushy brown hair sitting on the Epistle side of the main altar, near the tomb of Father Francisco García Diego y Moreno, first Bishop of California. The boy was emptying out the offering box, peering through wire-rimmed glasses to total up the money he was counting with an electric calculator.

"Excuse me," Sonny said. "I'd like to see a priest."

The young man had a sweet and guileless smile. "I'm a priest," he said.

Sonny's astonishment obviously showed.

"I really am," the priest said. "It's on my driver's license."

"No, I believe you," Sonny said, stopping the young man from reaching for his wallet. "It's just that you're so young."

"Yes, I am. I made a decision to serve God right after I got out of high school."

"You got a calling?" Sonny asked. A calling would be sufficient weight to offset a lack of experience.

The priest looked Sonny in the eyes, and smiled a little ruefully. "No," he said. "I can't say it was a calling. It was more like a whisper. Nothing like in the movies."

The sound of footsteps reached them, and the young priest craned his neck to investigate the visitors who had just entered the church. It was a small group, perhaps a sightseeing group, and Sonny realized that he had also been bothered by the interruption.

"If you'd like to see an older priest . . ." the young man was saying.

"No, no," Sonny said. "You'll do fine."

"I'll do fine for what?" the priest asked.

"I'd . . . I'd like you to hear my confession," Sonny blurted. Ten minutes before, he would have thought the idea laughable, but now, here in the Mission, it seemed so right, so inevitable.

"Really?" the priest said. He put the calculator down and closed the lid of the offering box. "I haven't heard many confessions," he confided. "In fact, you'd be my first."

"Your first?" Sonny said.

"In the field, I mean," the priest said hastily. "We practiced on friends at the seminary, but we all had such crummy little sins, barely worth confessing."

Sonny's impulse to laugh was so strong he could barely contain it. Nurses who looked like giraffes and owls; priests who looked like car hop waiters. But it wasn't funny—it wasn't funny at all.

"Maybe you *should* have a priest with more experience," the smooth-skinned young man was saying. "Father O'Hara will be here this afternoon. He's old."

"No, no! I can't wait," Sonny said. "So what if this is your first confession? It's my last. I'm a dying man."

"Dying?" The young man pronounced the word with horror, as if it had four letters instead of five.

"Dying," Sonny said.

The priest was opening and closing the lid of the collection box as if it were a cigar box that held baseball cards. "A lot of people say Father O'Hara looks just like Barry Fitzgerald," he said. "You know, kindly. A little twinkle in his eye . . ."

"Please!" Sonny reached out and took the priest's hand away from the collection box. "I need help now!"

The priest slowly rearranged Sonny's grasping hands, and suddenly he *was* giving Sonny comfort. Sonny's message had gotten through. "Certainly," he said, all business now.

"Thank you . . . Father," Sonny said, still having trouble with the idea. He looked directly into the young

30

man's eyes. "It's hard to call you Father, Father," he said.

The priest stood, carefully tucking the calculator into the collection box. "You can call me Dave if it's more comfortable," he said.

"Thank you, Dave," Sonny said.

The priest led the way toward the confessional and opened the door for Sonny.

"After you."

Sonny knelt in the confession cabinet and got himself comfortable. There was a slight pressure in his stomach, a threat of pain. He tried to forget what the young priest looked like, and attempted to compose his thoughts. He wondered if the young man was crossing himself and looking upward for guidance before entering the other side of the booth, and then he heard the door on the booth open and close and a rustle of clothing and then the noise of the sliding door on the little veiled window as it opened.

"Bless me, Dave, for I have sinned," Sonny said automatically, and then stopped in confusion.

"Dave?" he said.

"Yes?"

"I think I'd rather call you Father, Dave," Sonny said.

"Fine."

Sonny closed his eyes and began again. "Bless me, Father, for I have sinned."

"How long has it been since your last confession?"

"I asked myself about that before," Sonny said. "It's been twenty-two years since my last confession." And that's more years than you've been alive, he said to himself.

"Jesus Christ!" Dave's voice said, adding quickly, "Son of Our Lord, Blessed Member of the Holy Trinity." It made Sonny smile. There was a slight pause. "That's a long time."

31

Sonny could heard the priest rearranging himself: a rustle, as of papers.

"I was kind of hoping one of us would be good at this," David said, his voice rueful.

Sonny remained silent.

"Uh . . . Why have you stayed away from God's house so long?"

"I don't know," Sonny said, trying to be honest. "I guess I sort of stopped going to church when I discovered fuck . . . uh, sex."

"That's when we lose a lot of them," Dave said with absolute assurance.

"But I still believe in God," Sonny said hastily. "I mean, I'm still scared of Him, so I must still believe in Him, right?"

"Well, it's rather an odd way of stating your faith. But it *is* faith of a kind."

"That's right! I still have faith! And even if I don't, it can't hurt to make a last confession and do a little penance. Just in case there is a Heaven and Hell. I mean, it's like covering yourself both ways."

"We're talking about God, not craps," Dave said.

Sonny rubbed his hands on his cheeks. "Yeah, I know. I got the wrong attitude. This isn't going to do any good. That's why I quit praying. I figured if I didn't believe it, *He* wouldn't, either."

"We all lack faith sometimes. Every day I have questioned if I made the right decision . . . becoming a priest."

"Every day?" Sonny was truly startled.

"Every day since I was ordained."

"Every day since you were ordained?" What was he doing here listening to this teenager masquerading as a priest?

"Being a priest can keep a person from committing sin, but it can't keep a person from lusting after women, craving alcohol, dreaming of screwing a business partner—"

"Hey!" Sonny interrupted. "This is *my* dime. You're supposed to be listening to me!"

"I'm sorry," Dave said. "Please continue."

Sonny closed his eyes and desperately tried to bring up a vision of Father Conklin, who had heard the story of his first masturbation. Father Conklin had always reminded Sonny of his father, both being Irish, both burly, both with cheeks that would turn to jowls. Sonny had liked and respected Father Conklin. He had filled the confessional with his presence.

"I said you may continue."

"Sorry. Bless me, Father, for I have sinned. Among my most grievous sins are . . . uh . . . is jacking off still a sin? That used to be my biggie in the old days when I went to confession."

"Is that still your biggie?"

"No," Sonny said. "I'm an adult, and a parent, and I have been a rotten father to my daughter, Julie."

"Yes?"

Julie. How was he going to tell Julie? "I don't want to talk about that," Sonny said. That wasn't a mortal sin. "It's my mortal sins I should be confessing," Sonny said. "So there are a few things I have to get off my chest, Father."

"Yes?"

"I sell real estate," Sonny explained.

"Is that a sin?" Dave asked, real puzzlement in his voice.

There was no way to explain about any of the rotten deals—not Lake Crest Estates, or the deal with John Ashton, or even just the simple blockbusting. Dave would never understand. "Take my word for it," Sonny said. "The way I do it, it is. And another thing, all during my marriage, while I was ignoring my daughter, I was out fuck . . . copulating around with other women."

"You committed adultery during your marriage?" Dave said, with interest.

"Yes, I did, Father."

33

"About how many times?"

"Well . . . we were married eight years. I'd say about . . . two hundred times."

"Jesus Christ!" Dave said. "Son of Our Lord, Blessed Member of the Holy Trinity! Two hundred times?"

"Yes," Sonny said, checking his figures on his fingers. "About twice a month." He laughed. "How many Hail Marys do I have to say to make up for that?" His laughter was absorbed by the wood of the confessional's walls and faded into a growing silence. There was again the sound of rustling.

"Father, what are you doing?" Sonny asked.

"It's all right. Just a minute. I'm looking it up."

"Oh, Christ," Sonny said. "I came in here for help, and all I get from you is a punch line." He glanced at his watch. Nearly one o'clock. Time to go see Marty.

Sonny quickly released himself from the confessional. It was with a sense of finality that he stopped in front of the altar to kneel and quickly cross himself; then he headed for the sunshine outside the church, ignoring Dave, who had followed him, looking apologetic.

Oh, Lord. How was he going to tell Marty?

Chapter Two

THE CASA VEGA was a favorite hangout for Marty Lieberman, Sonny Lawson's lawyer and friend, and Sonny unerringly headed for the back booth of the cozy place that served the best margaritas in town. Darleen had definitely not been kidding when she'd said Marty was seeing a hot young thing, Sonny thought. The woman at Marty's table was in her twenties, a brunette, with a face that appeared to have Marty hypnotized. Sonny stood near the table for a second and watched his friend operate. He had reached out to take the brunette's hand.

"Filing for a divorce can be a very rough experience emotionally," Marty was saying. "I've always felt a lawyer should be at his client's side not only in the courtroom but wherever she might need him—at her home, the beach, my place." Marty noticed Sonny at this point and tried to send him on his way with eye daggers.

"I just want to make sure I get every cent I can out of Henry," the woman was saying. "I want to squeeze his balls dry."

"He must have hurt you very badly," Marty said, squeezing her hand by way of illustration.

"Marty, I have to talk to you," Sonny said.

The brunette looked up at him with appraising eyes; Sonny successfully fought an impulse to see if his moustache was in order, but was unable to keep him-

35

self from eyeing the magnificent breasts that pushed against the woman's hot-pink shirt.

"I'm in a business meeting," Marty said.

"Forget your cock," Sonny said, pulling his eyes away and pushing his way into the booth next to Marty. "I'm in real trouble."

"I'm sorry, Miss Bishop," Marty said to the brunette. "An old friend of mine. He takes liberties." Marty was attempting to kick Sonny under the table.

"Marty, I'm going to turn into a vegetable who shits all over himself!" Sonny said.

Miss Bishop quickly rose and slid out from her side of the booth. The rest of her figure was equally magnificent. "Well, you two friends just go ahead and chat. I have to get my legs waxed."

"Wait, Miss Bishop," Marty said, attempting to stand up and prevented from doing so by Sonny's presence in the booth. "Sonny, what the hell are you doing? That woman represents ten thousand dollars worth of business to my firm!" He pointed after the retreating woman. "And look at that ass!" With an effort Marty pushed Sonny out of the booth and started to follow Miss Bishop, but Sonny restrained him, holding onto the sleeve of his jacket.

"Marty, I'm dying," he said. So much for how to tell Marty. "I could go any second."

"What? What the hell are you talking about?"

"I'm talking about dying."

"What does that mean?"

"Dying means lying in the ground with a lot of dirt on top of you and holding your breath forever," Sonny said.

"I know what dying means. Oh, shit, she's gone. Well, come on, we might as well go back to the table and have lunch."

"It's going to happen to me. I went to a doctor today. He told me I was dying."

"They'll say anything to keep you coming," Marty

said, although the worry lines between his wide-set brown eyes deepened.

"No, no . . . it's true. I've got a toxic blood disease. I've known something was wrong for the last couple of months. I've been having terrible pains in my stomach and my chest. I'm nauseous and weak all the time."

Then Marty was looking at him, really looking at him, his brown eyes appraising, and Sonny could see him assessing the gray hairs that had proliferated in the last few months, and the weight loss which showed not only in his face but in the new notch in his belt and the sag in his trousers; and Marty's mouth grew tight around the lips, and he moved his head a bit on his neck as if the news had transferred itself into physical pain; and then Marty looked wildly around the room for a second, as if surprised to find himself still in the Casa Vega, before meeting Sonny's eyes again.

"I'm your best friend," Marty said softly. "Why didn't you tell me?"

"I did tell you," Sonny said.

Marty shook his head in wordless frustration.

"I've been telling you every time I've seen you for quite a while. The last time I was in your office, I threw up on your desk."

Marty took Sonny's arm and steered him out of the way of a waitress who was carrying a loaded tray to a foursome who greeted the appearance of their food with good-natured exclamations of appreciation.

"Come on, let's go back and sit at the table," Marty said.

They walked back to the booth in the corner and slid in, facing each other. Marty silently finished his margarita and then reached over and finished the drink Miss Bishop had left behind.

"What can I do, Sonny?"

"I want you to make sure my insurance policies and will and stuff are in good order, and that nothing from the business can touch the money. I want to be sure

everything is set for Jessica and Julie." Sonny toyed
with the silverware on the checkered tablecloth. "Oh,
God, I wish I hadn't gotten involved with Lake Crest
Estates, and that I hadn't pissed away the last three
years. If I'd just spent more time at the office, there'd
be more to leave Julie." The need to cry that had
threatened for several hours started a preliminary demand in his throat then, and Sonny pulled in a deep
breath and released a sigh so full of despair that a woman at the nearest table turned away from her food to
look at him.

"C'mon, Sonny, get hold of yourself." Marty's voice
was low-keyed but urgent. "You talk like you're going
to die tomorrow!"

No, Marty was wrong, Sonny thought. Marty of the
impromptu hundred-mile drive at two in the morning
to settle a bet about a stripper's boobs, Marty of the
weekend jaunts to the bullfights, Marty of the parties
at his friend's beach house, Marty of the clean-sheets-
on-the-sofa the night Jessica threw him out, Marty of
the irrepressible good humor . . .

"I'm going to die tonight," Sonny said with finality.
A massive pain had come; he pressed his palms flat on
the table to keep from moaning.

"What's happening, Sonny?" Marty said, his voice
clearly indicating his anxiety. "I don't understand."

Sonny shook his head, fighting to get himself under
control, motioning with his hand that he neded some
time to compose himself.

Marty signaled the waitress and ordered a couple
of margaritas, and he gave Sonny time, sitting silently
until the drinks arrived, gulping his down in two swal-
lows.

"I'm okay," Sonny said, pushing his drink across the
table to Marty, leaning back into the padded seat of
the booth, the pain in his stomach easing off.

"Please tell me what's happening," Marty said.

Sonny nodded. "Okay," he said. "What's happening

is that you're my lawyer and my best friend and I've got to tell someone and I'm telling you. I don't want to wind up in some hospital, curled up in pain, being kept alive by Blue Cross and electricity." And then, somewhat dramatically, because he wasn't yet sure if he had the courage, he said, "Marty, I'm going to commit suicide."

Marty's mouth opened as if he were going to speak, and then closed, as if speaking were more than his muscles could manage. He rearranged the silverware on the cloth in front of him and then picked up the menu, which he probably knew by heart, and studied it for a long moment.

"What do you think, Sonny? The enchilada plate?"

"Marty? Did you hear me? I'm going to—"

"Yeah, yeah, I heard you. Now I *know* it's all a big joke, right?" he said, his voice painfully hopeful. "It's all a joke, right?"

"No."

Marty started making tracks on the tablecloth with his fork. The action reminded Sonny of a movie he'd seen, many times, on the tube. But he couldn't quite place it. Ingrid Bergman? Gregory Peck?

"I've thought the whole thing over," Sonny said, thinking out loud. "I'm going to die anyway, and I don't want to live in all this pain." That was certainly true enough. "I'm going to knock myself off." How? How? "All it takes is a little guts to—"

"Guts!" Marty's voice was furious; he clattered the fork to the table. "You think running out on Jessica and Julie is a gutsy thing to do?"

"You bet! At least they'll collect some big insurance money instead of bankrupting themselves trying to keep me alive . . . preserving me like a goddamn pickle! You know what I did before? I went to the hospital and looked around, that's what I did! It's the world series of sickness up there on the terminal floor! You should have seen what I saw—the way they keep those wrecks alive with machines—"

"You think you're real smart," Marty said, interrupting, gesturing with his index finger like a parent lecturing a child. "You think you're real smart, don't you? But you forget one thing—your life insurance policy doesn't pay off on suicide. All the majors have a no-payoff clause on suicide. Ha, ha, ha . . ."

Marty's laugh was slow and deliberate, and Sonny found himself growing very quiet and grim. It was an idea—a *good* idea—and he was caught. The pain. He'd have to learn to live with the pain. Jessica could take care of herself—they'd been divorced long enough for him to know that. But Julie. He couldn't leave Julie without any money. He covered his face and shut his eyes and tried to think, but the pain was suddenly there again, there again. . . .

"Sonny," Marty said quietly. "Sonny, please stop. I can't see what you're doing under there. Are you crying, Sonny?"

Sonny heard Marty pick up the menu again, and then slap it down. "What do you think, the enchilada plate? Sonny, you won't be able to eat with your hands in front of your face." He reached over and tried to separate Sonny's hands, but Sonny repulsed him.

"Sonny . . . Sonny. . . . what should I do?"

What should he do? How was he supposed to know what Marty was supposed to do? Marty was supposed to tell *him* what to do. Sonny removed his hands from his face. He'd figure out what to do later, and at least Marty would begin to get his paper affairs in order.

"I'm okay, Marty," he said. " 'Bye."

Sonny slid out of the booth, but Marty caught his arm before he could leave the table.

"Wait!" Marty said. He was silent for a minute, looking at his friend. "Are you really in pain all the time?"

"Yeah," Sonny admitted. "It's okay. I'll call you later."

"I was lying about the insurance," Marty said quickly.

"What?" The statement seemed to flood his head with red.

"Yeah, I was lying," Marty said. "That suicide thing only applies during the first two years of a policy. They don't want guys signing up and then killing themselves right away for the money."

"You mean it?" Sonny said, a lightness invading him, more colors flashing at the edges of his brain.

"Yeah. You been with them ten years at least. You can do any goddamn thing you want to yourself, and they'll still pay you."

"Thanks, Marty. I'll see you, old buddy."

They shook hands, but Marty wasn't ready to let him go. "Wait a minute," he said. "Eat with me, Sonny."

"I haven't got much of an appetite."

"Have an enchilada. It couldn't kill you," Marty said, and then reddened with the almost instantaneous awareness of what he had said. "I'm sorry," he said, and then, realizing that no apology was necessary, "I . . . I'll make sure Jessica and Julie . . . make sure that they get everything."

"I know, I know." Sonny allowed himself to be maneuvered back to the table. The waitress, who had been watching them, walked over to take their order, but Sonny waved her away.

"How are you going to . . . do . . . to do it?" Marty asked.

"Sleeping pills," Sonny said with assurance. "It's the most painless. The only trouble is, I haven't got enough. Do you have any?"

Marty shook his head. "Just some Sleep-Eze. I don't think you can O.D. on Sleep-Eze."

"That's okay," Sonny said. "I'll find some." He

41

eased out of the booth once again. "I really have to go, Marty. I want to go over to Mary Ellen's place and say good-bye."

"Sure, pal," Marty said, and this time he let Sonny ease out of the booth without stopping him.

"Good-bye, Marty."

"Good-bye, Sonny."

But Sonny hesitated, as though Marty now had backed away. "One more thing, Marty . . ."

"Jesus, Sonny," Marty said, slamming down the menu. "You're really putting me through the wringer!"

"I want you to pay off the Jag, sell it, and give the money directly to Mary Ellen. My equity's worth about three thousand bucks. She deserves something for all the shit she's put up with being my old lady."

"Sure, sure . . . anything, Sonny."

" 'Bye." Sonny started for the door, but this time Marty stopped him. "Sonny," he said, "I just want you to know that I understand what you're doing. As a friend and a lawyer, I believe you have a legal and moral right to die any way you choose."

"Thank you for understanding," Sonny said.

And then Marty was grabbing for his shirt, and yelling, "Don't do it, Sonny!" His voice cut through the quiet of the restaurant, and diners at the other tables turned to look at him. "Stop this man," Marty said desperately to the faces that were watching. "He's about to—"

Sonny threw his arm around Marty's shoulders and got his neck down, and his hand in front of Marty's mouth, and walked him back to the booth, smiling at the curious faces that watched them.

"Now be my real friend, and when I uncover your mouth, just wave good-bye," Sonny said, unexpectedly letting go of Marty's mouth as a severe pain hit and he needed both hands to steady himself, to keep himself from sinking down. Marty was watching his face—he knew Marty was watching his face—but this time he

42

was silent. And then the pain eased and Sonny straightened back up and Marty was still silent, still watching him, and then Marty waved a small good-bye with his hand and sat down at the table and picked up a menu; and Sonny headed for the door, his ears listening for Marty's voice ordering the enchilada plate, as he had heard Marty's voice order the enchilada plate so many times before.

But this time would be the last.

And he left the Casa Vega and was out again in the beauty of the Santa Barbara day that wouldn't quit, and there was another ticket on the windshield of the Jaguar, and, yes, he thought, as he tore it up, today is my lucky day. The third ticket in less than four hours. And then, aloud, as if the small pieces of paper he scattered to the earth were a witness, "That's it . . . Marty's the last person I'm laying my shit on. I'm not telling Mary Ellen I'm dying."

But he did, of course, taking both her hands in his when she came to the door of her apartment, reaching out to kiss the skin of her beautiful cheek, saying, "Hey, I like that," to acknowledge the short, sash-tied kimono she was wearing which opened at the knees to expose her magnificent thighs and gaped in the front to show tantalizing glimpses of her golden melon breasts, and he put an arm around her waist and gently led her through the debris to the bed in the far corner of the large single room. The bed had broken under them a few months back, and Sonny had propped up the corner with telephone books, which were still there.

And he pulled Mary Ellen down on the bed with him, and held her tight, and told her, and listened to her sobs, and felt her sobs, and looked at the piles of paper, paper everywhere, and Mary Ellen's guitar propped against the wall and her music stand and sheet music, and the dirty dishes, and saucers of dried cat-food, and melted candles and garbage bags. Tabby was playing with the kitten on the couch she used as a scratching post. Against his chest Mary Ellen moved her immaculate body and sobbed, and now Sonny turned himself and pressed her against him, kissing the tears from her face, murmuring comfort and stroking, the feel of Mary Ellen's new robe good against his palms. He never understood how she kept herself so soft and clean and sweet in the face of the debris that cluttered her living space.

"Don't cry, honey, please don't cry. I'm sorry. I'm sorry I told you. Hell, I don't even care that much."

Mary Ellen stiffened at his words. "You don't care that your life . . . our life together . . . all the beautiful things we've shared . . . it's not true, is it? . . . Please . . ."

"Baby, come on," Sonny said, fighting with pain, with guilt, with passion, and then he was kissing her, kissing her deep, demanding that she match his intensity, backing off and becoming gentle with his tongue on her neck and down to the cleavage in her gown, his hands challenging the garment to protect her, prodding her, but Mary Ellen wasn't responding, wasn't ready, he was going too fast.

"Sonny, please . . . not now, not yet . . ."

"Would you deny me a last meal?" Sonny said.

Mary Ellen pushed at him, shoved at him, backing away on the bed. "You're . . . you're sick!" she said.

"It was just a joke," Sonny said, as far away from laughing as he could possibly be.

"It was terrible! You were actually trying to get me to respond by using your death!"

She was right, of course, and she was also very wrong, and Sonny let her go, so she could see it for herself.

"You're right," he said. "I'm disgusted with myself. I was going for a pity fuck. Can you imagine that?"

And like the little girl she was, Mary Ellen took pity on him then, throwing herself against him, her arms

44

wrapping him, her passion serious, and her robe had come loose in their frenzy to make each other happy, their desperation, and Sonny struggled with his clothes, laughing as Mary Ellen's attempt to help just slowed things down, and the potential for joy was there, and the things they had learned to do to and for each other got done, but a remoteness was with them, following Sonny even to his release, and it was there even after they had rested and temporarily had worn out the need to touch, and it was without a word that Mary Ellen finally rose and picked her way into the kitchen to fetch them wine.

Sonny never had learned to match Mary Ellen's total ease with nakedness in the kitchen, probably because the disorder there felt offensive to him, unlike the disorder in the big room. Sonny slipped into the kimono that Mary Ellen had discarded on the floor, and joined her in the kitchen.

His stomach was protesting vigorously.

She tied the sash at his waist and kissed his cheek.

He opened the refrigerator and found the milk on the shelf in the door. The glasses were all dirty, some in the sink, some on the table, filling up the spaces left over from piles of paper, books, Mary Ellen's typewriter, even a half-eaten TV dinner that might have been there for days. Mary Ellen had put some bakery rolls in the oven to heat, a haphazard procedure at any time, because her oven door had lost a hinge.

Sonny rinsed a glass and began to pour the milk. He made a face.

"How old is this milk?"

"I bought it at the market yesterday," Mary Ellen said.

"Then they must have got it from a dead cow," Sonny said, putting the milk back. "Do you at least have sugar for coffee? Preferably without ants?"

"There's some on the table," Mary Ellen said.

45

"Loose or in a bowl?" Sonny said, filling the kettle and putting it on the stove to boil.

"Sonny, why are you being mean?"

"I don't know," Sonny said. "I guess the news of my death put me in a bad mood."

Mary Ellen walked to him so naturally, so easily. Why couldn't he relax and accept her hug the same way? he wondered. But he could feel himself getting tense even as he willed his body to relax. He broke away from her and walked to the oven.

"How are the Danish coming?" he asked.

Mary Ellen used a hot mitt to open the oven door. She stuck a finger onto some icing and popped it in her mouth. "They feel done," she said. "It's hard to tell with this stove."

"Mary Ellen, the landlord would fix the stove if you asked him. He might throw you out when he sees this place, but he'd fix the stove."

"I'm going to call him," Mary Ellen said. "I've told you I'm going to call him." She took the tray of rolls from the oven and balanced it precariously on the edge of a stack of books on the table. Sonny automatically cleared a space on the counter for her to put the tray down, and then she found the paper towels, which were somewhere near the sink where Sonny could never find them, and a knife, which she wiped clean. Tabby and the kitten had joined them in the kitchen, hoping to be fed. It got Sonny annoyed to see the kitten sniffing at a can of dried food Mary Ellen had simply opened and placed near an empty water dish, and when Tabby jumped on the counter and sniffed at the sweet rolls, Sonny vented himself by knocking the cat to the floor. He could see Mary Ellen bite off an angry retort; she gave Tabby a little pat of comfort and began to cut the rolls, handing one to Sonny with a paper towel, then making them instant coffee with water that had not quite reached the boil.

"How was it in there?" Sonny said, nodding to the

bedroom and hiding his discomfort behind a sip of coffee and a bite of roll.

Mary Ellen shrugged. The movement made her breasts move, and Sonny restrained an impulse to reach out and stroke her. "It felt good," she said.

"Did you come?" he said. It was an old and sore point with them, and Sonny knew the answer before Mary Ellen shook her head with an embarrassed "No."

"There was a moment there," Sonny said, suddenly feeling mean, "when you let out a little gasp and sort of arched your back. I thought maybe you had an orgasm then."

Mary Ellen nibbled at her lower lip, and looked him in the eyes, and then looked away. Again she shook her head.

"Don't you remember, honey? You arched your back. It was just before—"

"I don't want a blow-by-blow description of our lovemaking, it takes everything away from it," she said, softening her words by reaching out and straightening the lapel of her kimono, which Sonny had managed to put on inside out.

"Yeah, you're right," Sonny said, taking another sip of coffee and gesturing toward her with the cup, "but maybe you had a little orgasm and didn't even know it."

Mary Ellen shrugged. "It's possible," she said.

"No, it's not," Sonny said, suddenly wishing that she would get dressed, cover her magnificent body, feeling inadequate, as he almost always did after their lovemaking, by his inability to make her climax. "Did you at least like it?"

"Of course I liked it, Sonny. I wouldn't do it if I didn't like it."

There was no guile in her face, nothing but honesty and beauty and truth, and Sonny knew she wasn't lying.

"Yeah," he said, "that's the difference between you

and me. *I've* done it to people I didn't like. I've done it to people nobody liked."

"Why do you keep coming here, Sonny?" Mary Ellen was saying, and Sonny realized that she was close to tears and that, inexplicably, he was getting angry. "I've told you exactly how I feel. Why do you keep coming here?" she said again.

And just as suddenly his anger—even his interest in the discussion—was gone and he was left feeling . . . not numb, exactly, because there was the pain in his stomach, but without any desire to remain here even one minute longer.

He shrugged. "I don't know why I keep coming here, Mary Ellen. Maybe I love jacking off." And then, before the impact of what he had said could reach her, he quickly drew her into his arms and kissed her cheek. "I'm going to get dressed and go now."

"Go where?" Mary Ellen asked.

"I want to see Julie, once before. . . ." Before what? Before he really did what he knew he was going to do?

"Before what?" Mary Ellen said, drawing back into the circle of his arms.

"Before . . . I have to tell her the bad news," Sonny finished lamely.

"You said you hadn't decided whether to tell Julie or not earlier, when you were telling me."

Sonny disengaged his hold on Mary Ellen and walked back into the bedroom, sorry that he had taken his coffee cup with him, eventually putting it on the floor near the head of the bed. "Look, I've had a traumatic experience, and I want to see my kid," he said.

"Don't get mad at me, Sonny," Mary Ellen said. "I just wanted to make sure you weren't thinking of doing something crazy."

"Like what?"

"I . . . I don't know," Mary Ellen said hesitantly, afraid to voice her fears. "Just, please, *please* don't do anything crazy."

"I won't," Sonny said. And then, nonchalantly, "Say, where's that gun I gave you to protect yourself?"

"Sonny!" Mary Ellen said, and fear was in her voice.

"I was just kidding," Sonny said hastily.

"Well, you're not funny," Mary Ellen said. Her hands bunched into fists but remained near her thighs.

"Yes, I am," Sonny said.

"No, you're not."

And then Sonny crossed his eyes, and arranged his mouth in a lopsided grin, and grabbed the hem of the kimono and did a little two-step shuffle, his right foot toeing out like a little girl ballerina, and Mary Ellen was laughing despite herself; and they were in each other's arms again, hugging, the comfort nearly unbearable, and then Sonny was gently holding her away from him, and then he drew her back for one more kiss, one more caress, before taking her firmly by the arm and planting her a safe distance away.

"I gotta change clothes, honey," Sonny said. "It embarrasses the kid when I pick her up in women's clothes."

"I don't know," Mary Ellen said. "I just hate to let go of you." She took the kimono that Sonny discarded, turned it right side out and slipped into it, tying the sash neatly around her waist. Sonny had donned his slacks and shirt but was having trouble finding his socks.

"Will I see you later tonight?" Mary Ellen asked.

"Uh . . . Yeah," Sonny said. "Sure." He found his second sock mixed up with the sheet that had been kicked onto the floor.

"Sonny, you're sure you're not going to—" Mary Ellen's words broke off at this point, and Sonny knew that she was worried, that she didn't quite trust or believe him, and then she finished up, "You're not going to do anything to yourself?" And she was looking at him with wide eyes, and her beautiful body was even sexier in the kimono than it had been naked, and he had to leave.

"Honey, I am *not* going to kill myself. You know me. If I was going to do something awful like that, I would have laid it on you by now."

Mar Ellen believed him and said so. "That's true," she said, and Sonny kissed her on the top of the head and feigned a boxing jab at her pert nose, and left the apartment wondering what she saw in him, a thirty-nine-year-old divorced man with a thirteen-year-old daughter; he complained about the way she kept house but never helped her, and he never gave her an orgasm, either.

And then, of course, there was Jessica.

There was always Jessica before there was Julie.

Sonny thought about that on the drive over from Mary Ellen's apartment. He had still not come to terms with the feelings that assailed him each time he drove into the cul-de-sac and stopped the Jaguar before the truly lovely house in which he and Jessica and Julie had lived together when they were still a family. Divorced for three years, out of the house for more than that, and still it gave Sonny queer feelings to come here. Well, he wouldn't be coming again, and so what if the thought was maudlin. He was allowed one maudlin thought for the day.

Slowly, over the years, with surprising economy, Jessica had managed to change the feeling of the house. When Julie was very young there was no doubt that the house said, A family lives here; and then somewhere about when Julie was eight or nine it began to say, A man and woman and child live here; and then Sonny moved out and the house said, A man *was* living here; and then that changed, too, until it said, There is room for a man here; but no one stepped in to fill the space Sonny had left, although Jessica dated a great

THE END

deal, and now the house said, A woman lives here who knows what she is doing.

Sonny pulled the Jaguar to the curb before the house. He didn't bother to lock it, and he entered the house without knocking, using the key that was kept on the ledge.

The house was quiet and seemed to be empty, but that had become Jessica's way.

"Hello!" Sonny called.

There was an immediate movement in the bedroom upstairs, the staccato sound of shoes with heels, and then Jessica came to the top of the stairs, her dark hair caught in a bun at the nape of her neck, several thin curls which were longer than her haphazard bangs framing her face and softening the severity of the hairstyle. She was wearing a simple white dress, with a single necklace with a large, intricate bauble on it that fell to a perfect place on the draped bodice. She was wearing artful makeup, and her legs were tanned and shapely and her ankles in her high-heeled sandals still caught his eyes, and Sonny found himself measuring himself against this lovely woman who had been his for as long as he had wanted; he felt himself a failure in comparison.

"Oh, shit," Jessica said, annoyed as she was always annoyed when Sonny let himself into the house without knocking.

"Hi, Jessie. Where's Julie?"

"The same place she's been every Wednesday afternoon for the last five years, ballet class. Why don't you ever remember that?"

"I didn't even remember it was Wednesday afternoon," Sonny said, watching her descend the stairs, so effortlessly, so much in control.

"What do you want, Sonny?" Sonny caught a trace of perfume, something new, something else she'd changed. "I'm about to go out on a date, and I have

51

to make Julie's dinner." She continued on past him toward the kitchen, not even stopping to be sociably polite.

Sonny followed and watched as Jessica concocted a one-serving meat-and-vegetable dish and put it in the microwave oven, setting the timer and cleaning up after herself as she went.

"Who are you going out with?" Sonny asked, taking the carrots from her and returning them to the refrigerator.

"None of your business. What are you doing here?"

"I told you. I want to see Julie." And then, without warning, he gave her a quick hug and nuzzled his face in her neck. "A date, huh? Since when do you like it in the afternoon?"

"Since I started working nights," Jessica said, pushing him away and cleaning the immaculate counter top with an equally immaculate sponge.

"So who told you to go to work teaching English at night?" Sonny said.

"The Bank of America. You think we can live in the style you got us accustomed to on your alimony? Which, by the way, you are six weeks behind on."

"I know, I know," Sonny said. "Things have been a little slow at the office."

"Maybe they'd speed up if you showed up there once in a while. They called here twice today looking for you. Have you told them you haven't lived here in three years?"

"Yeah, yeah," Sonny said, dismissing the topic. "Do you have any sleeping pills?"

"No." Jessica gave him a thoughtful look. "What do you need those things for? If you'd go on a healthy diet, cut out all the sugar and caffeine—"

"If I cut out sugar and caffeine, I'd starve," Sonny said. "And don't give me lectures from classes you took on my money."

"I was just trying to help," Jessica said with a shrug. Her tits didn't move, and Sonny wondered if she was wearing a bra; the soft drapery of the dress didn't let him tell.

"You relate everything to money," Jessica said.

"A little trick your lawyer taught me," Sonny retorted.

"Get out," Jessica said. "I am not going to let you spoil my afternoon." She made work for herself at the table, turning her back on Sonny.

"I'm sorry, Jessie," Sonny said, suddenly tired of it, tired of everything, tired of. . . . "I'm sorry, Jessie, I don't want to fight."

"You don't?" Jessica said with sarcastic surprise, but she looked at Sonny then, and her tone changed, and anxiety colored her words. "What's wrong, Wendell?" she said.

Sonny's tongue was pushed against the inside of his lips, which had pursed shut and would not open to let words out.

"If you're really having trouble going to sleep, borrow a couple of pills from your folks . . . they're hypochondriacs."

"They are not!" Sonny said. "You'll say anything against them." Then, as if it had been his idea, he said emphatically, "My folks will have downs."

"Why did you come here?" Jessica said.

"I want to talk to Julie. But . . ."

"But what?"

"But I guess there is something I should tell you."

"Will it depress me?" Jessica asked.

"I hope so," Sonny said, and even to him the words sounded nasty.

"Tell me tomorrow," Jessica said. "I've had a terrible day. Julie woke up at five o'clock in the morning screaming the shark was after her again." Sonny identified the look she gave him as a glare. "I'll never forgive you for taking her to that movie. You know she's afraid of the water, anyway."

"I'm sorry, Jessica, honest. I thought she'd love it. She said she wanted to go."

"Oh, Sonny, she'll say anything to look brave to you, don't you know that yet? You're so dumb."

Sonny banged his fist down on the counter. "I am tired of being told I'm dumb by people I'm supporting!"

"Don't yell! The maid's taking a nap."

"I support her, too!" Sonny yelled.

"Sonny, if you wake Maria—"

"Maria? I thought you fired Maria."

"This is another Maria. Julie's yelling woke *her* up at five o'clock, too. Then Maria started crying because she thought it was the Department of Immigration. After that, I just hung around with nothing to do until seven o'clock when I had to take Julie to school. I got back here about eight-fifteen, and Maria handed me a note from the washing machine man . . . he'd come to fix the washer, but nobody was home."

"Where was Maria?" What was he doing here, standing in this kitchen that wasn't his, having this inane conversation?

"She hides when anybody knocks at the door."

Sonny could not think of a single thing to say.

"Do you know how long I have been waiting for the washing machine man, Sonny?"

Sonny shook his head.

"Six weeks," Jessica said, spitting the words as if Sonny had been responsible. "We have no clean clothes. Yesterday I sent Julie to school in some of *your* old things." She raised the arm of her dress. Yes, she was definitely wearing a bra. "Smell this," she said.

Sonny shook his head weakly.

"I have waited days, *weeks* for this washing machine man. I've broken dates, missed appointments, I've even put out little snacks and candles for him. But he never comes . . . *he never comes!* Today I'm gone for a half hour at dawn, and he shows up! When I got home and heard that, I lay down on the bed, cried, and dreamed of moving to Paterson, New Jersey."

"What?" Sonny said.

"That's where the washing machine factory is. I figure they must have a few extra repairmen there . . . you know, trainees with spare time. If I lived near the factory, maybe I could get one to run over on his lunch hour or something and fix the goddamn machine!"

She looked at Sonny for several seconds, waiting for him to react, and when he didn't she pushed past him and headed for the pad of notepaper and the pencil always ready near the wall phone.

"You call that trouble?" Sonny said, finding his tongue, following her. She was writing a note to Julie— *Dinner in the oven, hugs, Mom.* "I'll tell you about trouble. About heartbreak."

Jessica picked up a strange little piece of obviously misshapen metal. "This fell off yesterday," she said.

"You're not listening to me," Sonny said.

"I don't have to listen to you," Jessica said. "You gave up that privilege when you walked out that door."

"I didn't walk out. You threw me out."

"With two hookers!"

"Jessie, I've apologized for that a thousand times. I thought you were of town. And we never got on our bed. I wouldn't do *that* to you."

"Yeah, Sonny. You always had class," Jessica said. She pointed out the kitchen window. "My date's here," she said, and then there was a knock at the front door and the sweet chimes of the doorbell, as if the person asking entrance wore both belt and suspenders, and Jessica was trying to lead Sonny to the back door.

"Get out, Sonny!" she said.

"No," Sonny said, an intense jealousy flooding him that he made no attempt to control.

Jessica made a snorting noise of disgust which on her looked good, and breezed out of the kitchen. Sonny followed her nonchalantly, and his surprise at the extremely good-looking, well-dressed young Latin man who unexpectedly stepped through the door couldn't have been greater. He gave a *whoosh*-ing sound through his moustache that caused Jessica to glance quickly in his direction.

"Déjame coger mi swéter; yo regreso en sequida. No presta atención a ese shmuck," she said, pointing at Sonny. She gave the young man a smile and a pat on the arm and walked to the stairs. "Be civil to Arthur or you'll pay," she gritted through her teeth at Sonny, and then the sound of her heels vanished in the carpet on the stairs.

Arthur was standing easily by the door, eschewing the hall chair, and he nodded pleasantly at Sonny.

"Hi," Sonny said.

"Hi," Arthur said, watching Jessica's ass.

"I'm dying," Sonny said.

"Yo no entiendo inglés," Arthur said, looking at Sonny now.

"Oh?" Sonny said. "You don't speak English."

The response was an enormous smile that showed even, white teeth, and the signs of expensive dentistry.

"You like screwing my wife?" Sonny said pleasantly.

Arthur shrugged, beginning to feel uncomfortable, sensing that Sonny was being aggressive, but unable to express himself.

Sonny shrugged back. "That's the way I felt about it, too," he said, and then Jessie was back, a sweater around her shoulders, a soft, touchable-looking sweater, and she was talking to the young man.

"Está bien. Vamos!" she said, and her arm went to tuck in Arthur's, as if she expected Sonny to allow her to breeze away like that.

"I want to talk to you, Jessica," Sonny said, taking her other arm, grabbing harder than he had intended, and Jessica stopped but did not attempt to free herself, not wanting to risk a scene.

"Por favor, espera en el auto," she said, and Arthur nodded politely, appraising Sonny with a look that was partial understanding and partial warning, and he made a graceful exit.

"Let go of me right now," Jessica said as soon as Arthur was out of earshot, and her voice carried such controlled fury that Sonny obeyed.

"Where are you and Pancho going . . . lunch at Taco Bell and a cockfight?"

"You are a racist ass, and we are going to a French restaurant you'd never take me to. Then we're attending an 'est' seminar."

"Bor-ring!" Sonny said.

"Not to me, Sonny. I'm trying to make my life a little better. It probably won't work, but at least I'm trying."

"Where'd you meet that greaser?"

"That 'greaser' is the son of a wealthy Argentine diplomat. He's in my English class, and you are still a racist ass." She tried to push by him, but he stopped her, running his hand down her arm, reaching for her breast. Yes, she was wearing a bra.

"And now the teacher is going to give her student a little tea and sympathy and jump his bones," he said.

"You are also a sexist ass," she said, slapping his hand away.

"The guy's ten years younger than you! You look like his chaperone!"

"How dare you say that to me! You're going out with a girl who still plays jacks! Now get out of my way or I'll spit in your face!"

"I . . . you wouldn't . . . I'm not finished talking to you—I have some important news."

"Get out of my way," Jessica said, and Sonny stepped out of her way because she had puckered up her cheeks, and her intensity was furious, and she was going to spit . . . and he let her go, and he had the guts not to tell her, to let her have the afternoon, because he had never fought fair, because he loved her, and because Julie was going to need her.

Chapter Three

JULIE HAS BECOME VERY BEAUTIFUL, Sonny thought, and she is nearly a woman. The awareness was bittersweet. Her breasts were fleshing out, taking on shape. Like the other young teenaged girls, she was wearing a leotard and tights. Her body was so supple, so healthy.

Sonny stood just outside the doorway of the main salon of Mistress Northrup's Ballet School, which was housed in an old two-story stucco building just a ten-minute drive from the house in the cul-de-sac, watching Julie and the other girls dance on the polished hardwood floor. The class was rehearsing to Beethoven's Fifth Symphony, music that even now reminded Sonny of Ann "The Lips" Martin, the girl from Brookline, Massachusetts, who had moved to the neighborhood his sophomore year in high school. She had sat next to him in Music Appreciation, and Sonny had written her a note and asked her out for a Coke while the Fifth was playing, the first day of class. How old had Ann been? Three years older than Julie? Four? Such kisses they had shared! Hours they had spent kissing! It had been as sweet as the dance the girls were now doing, but nowhere near as innocent.

Julie and a partner were now moving toward the center of the dance floor, away from the rest of the girls, their body and arm movements becoming broader, reminding Sonny of the gymnastics competitions he had watched during the Olympics, the snakelike arm movements on the balance beam, and the graceful moves of the free exercises without the somersaults and flips and cartwheels.

The dance mistress—Olga Northrup, Sonny remembered, was her name—stood to the left of the door, her hand resting on the barre, but Sonny could see her in the mirrors that covered the facing wall. She was dressed in a black short-sleeved shirt and black pants, and she stood perfectly erect and motionless, except for the fingers of her right hand, which played with her full bottom lip.

"Do not stop, girls, but Julie and Maria, you must loosen up even more here at this point. Use pelvic movements."

The acoustics of the room brought Mistress Northrup's voice clearly to Sonny; she was now giving almost constant direction to the girls, and Sonny found himself growing at first annoyed and then disturbed as the tenor of the dance changed, somehow leaving innocence behind and becoming sensuous. His daughter and her partner were circling each other, indicating attraction, teasing, coming together and dancing apart, touching, drawing attention to their bodies, occasionally doing movements that Sonny had seen in striptease bars but never in a ballet dance, and he realized suddenly that he had been watching mesmerized, that he was shocked, that now Julie and the girl she danced with were simulating an act so sexual, so explicit, that he was responding like a man, and it frightened him, angered him.

He walked through the door into the salon. Julie was engrossed in the dance. He was glad that she had become professional enough, enough of a performer, so that his presence did not cause her to lose her concentration, although he also wanted her to stop.

"What are you doing here?" Mistress Northrup asked, disengaging her hand from the barre. She was a stern-looking woman with a handsome face that was aging very well. "You're not supposed to be here, you know."

Sonny pointed to Julie, who was now slowly entwining her arms around her partner, bending her back across her arm.

"I'm her dying father," Sonny said.

"What?"

"That one's my daughter, and I would like to know what they are doing!" Julie was slowly executing a series of movements that looked as if she were attempting to mount her partner.

"It's a modern interpretive dance," Mistress Northrup said.

"Of what?" Sonny could feel heat rising toward his collar. Miss Northrup was twisting a large gold-braided ring which she wore on the index finger of her left hand.

"It's called 'Movement of the Bunnies.' "

"Bunnies? Like in rabbit?"

"Of course."

"What are the bunnies supposed to be doing?" Sonny said, knowing that he had raised his voice, but then Beethoven had gotten louder also. "Or shouldn't I ask?"

"They're doing whatever bunnies do in their wild state—"

"But both those rabbits are girls!" Sonny protested, outlining the shape of their figures with his hands in case Miss Northrup didn't get the point, wanting to ring the woman's neck for allowing—no, insisting!—that Julie move her body in that way.

"That's because we do not have any male dancers to portray the male bunny," Miss Northrup said.

Sonny opened his mouth to speak, but couldn't find words, and then he was watching Julie again, and his anger erupted and he could no longer contain his fury.

"That isn't ballet," he yelled, "it's smut!"

"You are a buffoon!" Miss Northrup said, glaring at him with eyes like ice. Julie and her partner had continued with their dancing, but some of the chorus girls had stopped moving and were now watching the adults.

"Break, girls," Miss Northrup said, lifting the needle from the record. "Julie, do you know this person?"

"My dad," Julie said.

"Julie, get your things, I want to talk to you," Sonny said.

Julie looked at Miss Northrup in confusion.

"That's all right, dear," Miss Northrup said, and Julie shrugged and left her place. "Is anything wrong, Dad?"

"No. Just get your things."

"Sure, Dad." She smiled at him like a good little girl, but made a fist that only he could see as she went to retrieve her clothes and schoolbooks.

"I'm not paying for my daughter to learn this stuff, Miss Northrup," Sonny said when Julie was out of earshot.

"You're certainly not," the ballet mistress said. "Her bill hasn't been paid in months."

Sonny took some mild satisfaction from the look of outrage that crossed Miss Northrup's face in response to the vulgar gesture he made with his arm and fist, and then Julie was back, a short skirt tied around her leotard, and he took her arm.

"You ready, honey?" he said.

Julie quickly headed out of the salon, waving goodbye to a couple of the girls, but obviously embarrassed and glad to get him out of the class. "What are you doing here in the middle of the afternoon?" she asked when they were outside.

"I missed you," Sonny said, "and I had a sudden impulse to go play miniature golf."

"Miniature golf?" Julie said, her voice wailing off into the afternoon. She was looking in the direction of a trio of boys who were lounging near a Catalina convertible. The looks they gave Julie did nothing to improve Sonny's disposition.

"Haven't you got a coat or something you can wear over that leotard?"

"It's hot. Quit being silly," Julie said, and Sonny realized that she knew what he was talking about, and that disturbed him, too.

"Okay," he said. "Come on, let's go."

"Not until you tell me what's wrong," Julie said.

"Nothing's wrong. Just a father taking his daughter out for an afternoon of miniature golf and a chat. No big deal. Nothing special." Even to himself Sonny sounded silly, but the idea had come to him quite suddenly, and he knew it was a good thing to do, just as he had a sudden feeling that today he must tell Julie about life, not death, and that that might be even harder.

Julie had been looking at him intently, and now she shrugged and reached out to touch his moustache, and the shrug brought Sonny's eyes to her breasts again, and that reminded him of the boys near the curb, who were still watching Julie, looks on their faces that Sonny knew he was reading accurately; and hastily, before Julie changed her mind, he got her settled in the passenger seat of the Jaguar.

"Why are you taking me to play miniature golf, Dad?" Julie asked, giving the boys a wave as Sonny drove out of the ballet school's parking lot.

"I don't know," Sonny said. "It would be nice to play, and I feel like buying you something silly, like a hat with 'Daddy's Girl' on it, or some cotton candy, or a frozen banana, or a hot dog. Are you hungry?"

"No, and you know I hate miniature golf."

"No, I didn't know that," Sonny said honestly. "You loved it the last time we played."

"That was six years ago, Daddy."

"The game hasn't changed," Sonny said. "Oh, the windmills and castles are a little fancier, but—"

"Daddy, *I've* changed," Julie said.

Sonny braked for a red light and really looked at his

daughter. Her hair was no longer light blonde, as it had been when she was a child, but was a honey color with wonderful highlights. She had inherited the shape of Jessica's face, and Jessica's high cheekbones, but the eyes he saw he knew were his, and so was the mouth with the slightly too-thin upper lip which Sonny compensated for with his moustache, and which kept Julie from being truly beautiful. But she smiled a lot, and had good teeth, and her skin was fantastic.

A horn sounded behind him to signal that the light had changed, and Sonny fondled his daughter's hair for a moment, then headed the Jaguar in the direction of the freeway.

"Yes, darling, of course you've changed," Sonny said. "You're thirteen now."

"Fourteen," Julie said. "I've been fourteen for half a year."

"Thirteen, fourteen, what difference does it make?" Sonny said. "It doesn't mean that we can't go have an afternoon like we used to have and just relive some memories."

"Sure, Dad," Julie said. "I didn't say I wouldn't go, I just said that I hate miniature golf."

"Well, try and forget that, and let's have a good time."

"Okay, sure," Julie said.

"Right," Sonny said. "We'll just have a good time. Why don't you find some music on the radio and just relax and enjoy the drive."

"Sure, Dad," Julie said.

Mild pain had started in Sonny's side, unfamiliar pain, heading for a spot in his back that was unreachable. It was just a twinge, really, but Sonny knew from experience that once pain found a new spot to test, it wasn't going to go away. He almost welcomed it because it was much less severe than the pain that had turned his stomach into an enemy; it was just an annoyance, really, for it did not make him sweat or feel nauseous or have to fight a desire to pull the Jaguar to the side of the road, and he wanted nothing to happen that would spoil the pleasant serenity he now felt, driving the Jaguar automatically, and Julie in the seat next to him looking relaxed and pleased with the Cat Stevens song that was coming from the radio. And then they were both joining in to sing "Yellow Submarine" with the Beatles, and Sonny thought, I'm not going to tell her, not today. I'm going to let myself have some fun, and his stomach growled then, with hunger, not pain, and Julie laughed because the noise had come audibly into the single second of silence between the end of the song and the announcer's raucous voice.

"You're hungry," Julie said.

"Yup, I'm hungry," Sonny said. "I didn't have any lunch." He pulled into the parking lot of a miniature golf course and paid their admission. "Come on, let's have a hot dog, and then I'm going to buy you that hat. Are you sure you're not cold in that thing?" he asked suddenly then, because they had passed two teenage boys and a man about Sonny's age, all of whom had given Julie the once-over.

"It's a hundred degrees out, Dad," Julie complained.

"Yeah, I know. Forget it."

But Sonny couldn't forget it, for the leers at Julie continued while they stood at the concession stand and ate hot dogs and washed them down with Coke, and while they waited for the seamstress to sew the words "Daddy's Girl" on a blue denim hat, and followed them out onto the miniature golf course itself, where Julie proceeded to beat him by nine strokes, forgetting herself as soon as she had the golf club in her hand, showing that she was having a good time and being enthusiastic about her shots. But Sonny's mood grew darker and darker, and when the pain in his stomach began to threaten—was it protesting the cotton candy or the frozen banana?—he had trouble talking Julie into quitting the game two holes early. She was grumpy

65

and a little annoyed with him by the time they returned to the Jaguar, pouting like the Daddy's Girl it said on her hat.

In the parking lot a car was disgorging a rowdy crew of boys from a beat-up Volkswagen, and Sonny hustled Julie into the front seat of the Jaguar. But not before the boys had noticed her and leered. Julie immediately took the hat off and stuffed it between the seat and the gear box.

Did we go around with leers on our faces all the time when we were teenagers? Sonny wondered suddenly.

Yeah, he answered himself grimly. We sure did.

Julie was stretching, her arms at shoulder level, her hands clenched in fists behind her neck, her movements constrained by the car's low ceiling.

"Julie," Sonny said, quickly starting the Jaguar and beginning the drive back to the house, "you're at an age when boys are starting to notice you."

"Sure, Dad, I know that," Julie said.

"Well, my dear, that's really why I came to see you today. It seems to me that it's time we had a talk about you . . . about your being a woman."

"Okay. Is there something in particular bothering you?"

What *was* bothering him, Sonny wondered. That she was growing up? A worry that some punk kid with pimples on his face was going to touch her? That she needed to protect herself? From what? Living? It was all so short, anyway. Too hard to find a way to explain. Where to begin?

He maneuvered the Jaguar around a white convertible with a hard-faced woman in her late thirties at the wheel. She was wearing a stretch jersey halter top that clung to her breasts so closely that Sonny could see the outline of her nipples. Was it his imagination, or were they actually beginning to. . . .

"Look, Julie," Sonny said, pulling his eyes away

from the convertible and easing the Jaguar onto the freeway. "Right now I want to talk about the way you're dressed. I don't mind your short skirt so much, but that leotard. . . ." He left the sentence dangling.

"I have to wear the leotard for ballet," Julie said, "but I like the way it makes me look, and it's very comfortable."

"It also makes your body very noticeable!" Sonny said. "So you should change after class." He could feel himself getting angry, partially at Julie, and partially at the unchangeable forces that made this talk—this visit—necessary. The white convertible had pulled alongside, and Sonny watched the blonde woman as she drove past, glancing over at him once with a speculative look on her face.

"Julie," Sonny said, "when you're dressed like that, even the winos start to leer at you. You really have got to be. . . ." What did she have to be? Eternally a child? Flat-chested, with a baby belly?

"Look, sweetheart," he said lamely, "thirteen is a dangerous age."

"I'm fourteen, Dad. I reminded you about that before."

"Okay. So fourteen is a dangerous age."

"So is forty," she said.

"I'm thirty-nine. Anyway, I want to talk about sex—not age," he said. "It's time we had a talk about sex."

"Well, if you want to talk about sex, I know plenty," Julie said.

Sonny was startled by the assurance in her voice. "You do?" he said.

"Sure. I'm at the top of my class in sex education. I just got an 'A' on my paper on menstruation."

"That's nice," Sonny said, and stopped talking for a moment because the woman in the convertible had fallen back down to his speed, and at another time he would have played the game, but not now.

"That isn't what you meant, is it, Dad?" Julie said.

"No, not really," Sonny said. "I'm talking about another kind of sex." And he almost brought the woman in the convertible to Julie's attention, but the car speeded up again and the woman did not glance at him.

There was a silence then, which Julie finally broke by reaching over and turning the radio on, but Sonny immediately turned it back off.

"No, wait, sweetheart, I really do want to talk. It's just that I'm having trouble figuring out exactly the right way to tell you what I want to say, because I don't want to make you automatically suspicious of the opposite sex the rest of your life."

And then he was looking at her from the corner of his eye, and in the inside lane a middle-aged, balding man had taken his eyes from the road to glance at Julie, just as he had looked at the woman in the convertible, and Sonny felt the words tumbling out.

"Julie," he said, in a tone that he realized sounded stern, "all boys, and that includes men, are filthy, rotten beasts with only one thing on their minds. They'll lie, cheat, commit violence . . . anything to get you in bed. Then they'll dump all over you."

Julie opened her mouth to respond, then closed it again and watched the landscape speed by for a while.

Finally she said, "You're not like that, Daddy."

"Yes, I am," Sonny said emphatically. "If you don't believe me, ask your mother."

"Well, I'm not Mom," Julie said, her voice less calm. "And things are different now."

"No, they're not," Sonny said. "It's always the same."

"And besides," Julie said, "what makes you think some stupid boy could trick me into doing something I didn't want to do?"

"We have our ways . . . even the stupid ones have their ways."

Sonny cut off the car driven by the balding man, then took the exit from the freeway and headed for the cul-de-sac.

"Why don't you worry that I could just as easily trick a boy?" Julie asked unexpectedly.

"Because boys want it more than girls," Sonny said.

"Not the ones I know," Julie said.

"They don't?" Sonny said, taken aback.

"No," Julie said.

Sonny threw up his hands. "This country is turning into a nation of fags!"

"Watch the car, Dad," Julie said, laughing. "You act so crazy sometimes."

Sonny leered at her, making the funny fish face that had always amused her as a child, and she laughed again, but then suddenly became serious.

"Why are you telling me all this now?" she asked, her voice troubled.

Why, indeed? Because a balding old man had looked at her breasts and it had made him angry? Because he had three months to live if he let nature take its course? Because the pain in his stomach was threatening again and he wasn't going to let himself turn into a white lump of a machine-fed vegetable?

And because he was on the verge of telling her the truth, wanting to tell her the truth, but unable to because he didn't know what the truth was, Sonny lied. "Well," he said, "there's another thing I have to tell you. Daddy's got to go away for a while."

Julie made a clicking noise with her tongue, pursing her lips together in a way that denoted displeasure, and she made a face at him, the same face she had made at him ever since she was a little child, a face that said he had betrayed her.

"When are you going?" she said.

"Today. I wish I didn't have to go, but I do." He reached out a hand and put it on her knee, and she squirmed around in the seat, and again Sonny was aware of how revealing the leotard was that she wore.

"Goddamn it," he exploded, "and if you have to

69

wear that thing except in dance class you should put on a sweater or shirt or something."

Julie snarled at him and shrugged his hand from her knee and said, "I'm glad we're almost home." Her voice was petulant.

There was a strained silence in the Jaguar for the remainder of the trip, Julie moodily keeping her face averted from Sonny, and Sonny feeling depressed about the turn of events that had taken place between them. Was it right? he wondered. Was he doing the right thing? Should he tell her, would she understand, would she support him or need support from him? Was it fair to keep it from her—did he dare hint that he might not be coming back? Did he have a friend with a garage where he could keep the Jaguar's engine running if his folks didn't have pills? What was Julie going to do?

And then they were in front of the house, and Julie turned a sad face toward him and sat still for a moment before reaching over to give him a peck on the cheek and then opening the door; but Sonny stopped her before she could leave, and awkwardly he pulled her toward him, giving her a hug.

"I'm sorry we had a fight, baby," Sonny said.

"Me, too," Julie said.

"Let's not be mad about anything between us . . . ever. Even things that happen in the future."

Julie drew away. "What do you mean?" she said, and Sonny knew he had made her uneasy. He didn't want to make her uneasy.

"Julie, there . . . there are some things in this old life that don't make sense when they first happen. People do things you might not understand until years later."

She looked at him quizzically. "You mean like *2001?*" she said.

"What?" He did not understand her.

"The movie," Julie explained. "When I first saw it,

70

I didn't understand it. But I went back last year and I did. Is that what you mean? Like *2001?*"

Sonny shook his head. "Not exactly," he said.

"Then I guess I don't know what you're trying to tell me, Daddy."

Of course, Sonny thought, how could she possibly understand when he wasn't telling her what he wanted to tell her—that he loved her and wanted to be there for her always, and that he wasn't going to be and he couldn't tell her that any more than he could keep her from growing up. And he was glad that he hadn't told her about his visit to Dr. Krugman or about the vague plans brewing in his head—glad that she, like Jessica, would spend the rest of this beautiful day feeling happy and secure and not worrying about their future.

"It's all right, honey," he said, "I was just trying to get serious for a minute because I'm going to miss you." He gave her a hard look, scrutinizing her face, but it was suddenly too painful for him. He wanted this meeting to be over because he was on the verge of losing control.

"Well, honey . . . I better go," he managed to say, clearing his throat, which had suddenly thickened. He kissed her and gently pushed her in the direction of the Jaguar's open door, but Julie stopped him.

"Is this a business trip?" Julie asked.

"Uh . . . yeah," Sonny said.

"Is Mary Ellen going with you?"

"Not this time." Mary Ellen would never be going with him again.

"Who's going to take care of you?" Julie wanted to know.

Sonny shrugged. "Guess I'll have to do it."

Julie leaned over and began to play with a button on the top of his open sports shirt. "I wish I was going with you," she said.

"Don't say that!" Sonny said, slapping her hand away.

"What's the matter?" And then, a sudden look of anxiety crossing her face, Julie asked, "Daddy, where are you going?"

"Bakersfield," Sonny said, off the top of his head.

"But you talk funny. Like you're going somewhere ... awful," she protested.

"Have you ever been to Bakersfield?" Sonny said, trying for a laugh, but Julie wasn't biting.

"I know you haven't been feeling good," she said. "Are you going into the hospital?"

"No, darling. You have my word. Daddy's not going into any hospital."

His sincerity must have been obvious, for relief surged into Julie's eyes. "I'm so glad," she said, kissing him.

"I'm going to miss you, Julie. More than anything, I'm going to miss you."

"You'll see me when you get back," she said, doubt on the verge of forming again.

"Yeah," Sonny said quickly to soothe her, knowing he wouldn't see her again, hugging her again, the tightness in his throat reaching up to his eyes now, tears forming, and he pretended to check the entrance of the cul-de-sac for traffic to keep his eyes averted.

"I've got to go, sweetheart," he said, and she stroked his shoulder and got out of the car, waving and calling to Martha, the girl who had recently moved into the house next door.

" 'Bye, Daddy," Julie said, and hurried off.

Eyes half-shut to cope with his tears, Sonny watched Julie run across the lawn and dump her books in the house and then as quickly come out and head for Martha's house; and Sonny knew it was going to be different but also bad at his parents' apartment, but not as bad as this. No, it wasn't going to be as bad as this.

And with a deep sigh, his tears under control, he wiped his eyes with the back of his hand, started the Jaguar down the street, and, at the exit from the cul-de-sac, he carefully perched the four-sizes-too-small hat he had bought Julie on his head, knowing she had left it behind deliberately because she hadn't wanted it in the first place, and he was glad she'd left it behind, very glad, and he knew he looked ridiculous, and he didn't care at all.

But he left the hat behind in the Jaguar, pushing it down next to the seat, as Julie had done, when he pulled up to the apartment building where his parents lived. He had taken the time to stop at a gas station and fill up the Jaguar and make a trip to the men's room, where he washed his hands and face and ran a comb through his hair. He had stood a minute looking at himself in the mirror. Not a bad face, he thought. It wasn't a bad face at all. He'd seen less interesting faces make it big in Hollywood; he'd scored plenty with his good lively lines and this face that looked pale to him now even with his tan. Yet it didn't look like the face of a man who had run out of time.

Clear eyes under heavy brows, and the furrows on the forehead could have come from artistic suffering instead of pain and worry. Good hair, a full head of dark brown, cropped hair—his father still had all his hair—but last week Sonny's barber had tentatively suggested coloring for the gray that had begun to sprout, noticeably so in the last few months. Straight teeth. Good teeth. Expensive-orthodontia-as-a-child teeth. Carefully trimmed moustache. He lifted the ends. Yes, the lines around his mouth were becoming permanent. Still, it wasn't a bad face. Not a bad face at all, for a coward.

No more thinking, Sonny thought, and rang the bell to his parents' apartment. He could hear the television set being turned down—his mother always turned the television set down when the doorbell or phone rang—and then Maureen Lawson opened the door.

"Hi, Mom," Sonny said.

"Sonny!" his mother said, glad to see him. She was wearing a flowered cotton housedress and beige slippers; her red-brown hair needed a touch-up. She was an attractive woman who had been beautiful, but Maureen Lawson had aged without grace. Sometime in the last few years she had given up all makeup, stopped wearing clothes that fit, and she had become a television addict.

Sonny gave his mother a kiss on the cheek and entered the apartment.

"Hi, Dad," Sonny called to his father, Ben, who was working on a paint-by-numbers picture at the dinette table, and when Ben Lawson turned around to smile his welcome, Sonny realized with a start that his father was getting old, was actually going to be seventy this year. Sonny had never thought of his father as *old*. The face had wrinkles, and the pouches had become permanent, but Ben's eyes still had the twinkle.

Sonny walked through the living room that always reminded him of polished agate eggs: there were gold flecks in the paint on the ceiling, gold flecks in the short-pile tweed rug, gold flecks in the material that covered the sectional couch and the matching easy chairs.

"What are you working on, Dad?"

"A painting called *The Potato Farmers*," Ben Lawson said. "It's by Vincent van Gogh. Only I don't like this guy's colors. They're all the same. All day I've been painting eleven, eleven, eleven. You hungry, son?"

"Oh . . . I'm almost out of milk," Sonny's mother said, already eager to return to her quiz program.

"That's okay. I'm not hungry. I just dropped in for a few minutes. Thought I'd see how the art world was going."

"It's boring," Ben said. "But what else are you going to do when you're my age? Sit around and watch your hands turn brown?"

"I hope you can stay awhile, Sonny," Maureen said, walking back toward the television. "We never talk."

She settled herself in the Naugahyde lounger and turned up the TV volume with a remote control device.

"Er . . . actually, I have to get back to work," Sonny said. "What I really wanted was to borrow a couple of sleeping pills. I . . . um . . . I've been working a lot, and it's hard to go to sleep when—"

"Sleeping pills?" his mother said. "We don't have any sleeping pills, do we, Ben?" Her face assumed a look of innocence.

"You know damn well we got enough sleeping pills in there to put the Mormon Tabernacle Choir in a coma," Ben said, giving Maureen a glance that was not friendly. "Take what you need, son. Careful how you use them."

"I will be," Sonny said. "Where are they?"

"In the bathroom."

"Don't take too many," Maureen called after Sonny. "So many young people are getting addicted to those things."

"Try the blue ones," Ben called. "They'll really put you in la-la land."

Like the rest of the apartment, Maureen kept the bathroom spotless. Her family hadn't been lace-curtain Irish for nothing. The medicine cabinet held an enormous variety of patent medicines and more than a dozen prescription pill bottles, and Sonny shook his head with surprise. No wonder his folks could put up with each other. Most of the bottles contained sleeping pills or tranquilizers, and Sonny took some from each bottle, counting them as he went. He took fifty, transferring his change to his left pocket and putting the pills in the right. He moved them around until the bulge wasn't too noticeable, but neither of his parents so much as smiled at him when he returned to the living room. Maureen was hypnotized by the television, and Ben had gone back to work on his painting.

He walked to his mother and kissed her cheek. "I really have to go."

" 'Bye dear," his mother said, giving him a quick glance with her large round eyes, and a quick smile.

"Sure you're not hungry?" Ben said, leaving his painting. "We got great meat loaf."

"Gee, I'd have to heat it up," Maureen said, obviously reluctant to leave her show.

"Think you could handle it?" Ben said sarcastically, "or would you like me to call in extra help?"

"I only meant—"

"That's okay," Sonny broke in, not wanting to get involved in one of his parents' squabbles, surprised because his father's voice had suddenly reminded him of Father Conklin. He wondered what they would say if he told them about his confession this morning. "I'm not hungry, honest. See ya." He headed for the door.

"See ya," Ben said.

But it wasn't as easy as Sonny thought, opening the door and leaving his parents, and he found himself with his hand on the knob, looking back into the room, a surge of feeling preventing him from taking what suddenly felt like a final step. Perhaps, if he told them, they could. . . .

"Is something wrong, Sonny?" his mother asked, and now it was Ben who sensed that his peace was about to be disturbed, and a shadow fell in his eyes and Sonny could actually see him withdraw.

"Of course there's nothing wrong," Ben said hastily, to cut off any further conversation. He began to put the tops on his paints.

"Well," Sonny said, "There is something—"

"Something wrong?" Maureen said, concerned enough to lower the volume on the television.

"No, Maureen," Ben said, not wanting to hear disturbing news. "Leave him alone."

Sonny closed the door and came back into the living room. It didn't feel like home. Nothing had felt like home after Ben and Maureen had sold the house and begun to live in apartments.

76

"I guess there is something I should tell you," he said, watching his mother and father exchange glances. He had never told them anything important since college, and he was quite certain that they liked it that way.

"I . . . I went to the doctor today and I'm . . . sick. Real sick," Sonny said.

"Damn," Ben said, getting up from the dinette table. "I need some number eleven. Burnt sienna. This guy uses a lot of burnt sienna. Maybe I left it in the bedroom." And without looking back at Sonny or Maureen, Ben went into the bedroom.

Sonny watched his father go, wondering why he still could feel hurt and bewilderment at his father's inability to give him support when he needed it. But then it had always been that way—his dad was there for him when he was feeling good and had good news to share, but not when he needed moral support, and his mom was there when the going got rough only up to a point. It wasn't actually such a bad arrangement, Sonny thought. Some parents couldn't even share the happy news. They had never abused him physically, and they had never tried to impose standards of behavior on him other than insisting that he go to church as a boy, and while he had stopped telling them the truth about his life in his teens, he had never actually *had* to lie to them, either, except when he felt like it. But this was different, and. . . .

No, he realized suddenly, he wasn't going to tell them. *Couldn't* tell them. Not with a pocket full of their pills, not when his mother would tell his father later, using the news like a weapon, letting Ben have the chore of checking the pill bottles.

"It's not really that bad, Mom," he said. "I may need to get a shot or something." He tried to keep his voice light, but his mother was still taking him seriously.

She turned down the sound on the television one more click and shook her head to disagree with his statement. "It's more than that," she said. "You haven't been looking well to me lately." She reached out to feel his forehead and led him to the couch, sitting next to him and taking his hand.

"Mom, I haven't looked well to you since I got out of junior high." Besides, he added to himself, you haven't really looked at me since you got your first television set. "It's nothing, really."

"Sonny, tell me the truth," Maureen said, and Sonny could see by her eyes that she knew he was lying. "I'm still your mother. What kind of sick are you?"

"Well . . ." Sonny knew she would persist in her questioning and that it was probably easier to just blurt out the truth, to repeat to her what Dr. Krugman had told him, but something kept him from doing it. He could hear Ben slam a drawer in the bedroom. He hedged.

"I've been having some pains . . . mostly in my chest and stomach," he said truthfully, "and some pretty bad headaches," which wasn't exactly true, but she would relate to the headaches. "I'm weak a lot, too," he said as an afterthought.

And he watched with some strange clinical detachment as his mother's eyes grew wide with terror. "Oh, Sonny," she said in a high, tense voice. "I know what that is!"

"Now, Mom," he started to say, sorry he had come back into the apartment.

"I have the same thing!"

"What?" Had he heard her correctly?

"I wake up in the morning and just want to stay in bed. Do your pains come mostly on the left side?" She pointed to an area of her abdomen slightly to the left and below the bottom of the rib cage.

"No . . . no . . . they're kind of spread out evenly," Sonny said, and even as he said the words the pain in his stomach began, a slight, dull ache that he knew would turn into a hot, raging stab in minutes. Hastily he got up from the couch. "I really have to go back to work, Mom," he said.

"You stay with the doctor, Sonny," Maureen said, leaning over and turning the sound back up on the television.

"I will."

"And ask him about my pain on the left side."

"Okay, Mom." He gave her a quick kiss on the cheek. "And say good-bye to Pop."

"Sure, Sonny," she said.

Sonny shut the door behind him firmly.

Chapter Four

AT SOME POINT during the two hours since he had returned to his apartment, Sonny had begun to talk to himself out loud. Simple sentences, spoken in a normal conversational tone, as if the mechanical chores he was performing needed an audible accompaniment.

"I'm running out on my kid."

He knew that he had said that sentence at least once before. It had been the first one he'd voiced. Had he said it in the shower, or earlier, while washing the glass top of the coffee table in the living room before carefully emptying out his right-hand pants pocket of its cache of pills?

It had taken him ten minutes to arrange the pills in a pattern that suited him the first time, the nine Seconal from his own medicine cabinet giving him a terrible fifty-nine to work with. Nothing little divides into fifty-nine. He wasn't sure anything divided into fifty-nine. So he sorted the pills and capsules according to size and color and arranged them in straight rows with spaces between to compensate for the size differences, and then he took one of the blue ones his father had recommended to make things all a nice simple even number, but he didn't like the way the two long rows of twenty-nine each looked, even when he interspersed big and little ones, yellow and red ones, punctuating with the capsules.

"Ahh, she's probably better off without me," his voice said, "and if you take one of the red ones and one of the capsules, you will have fifty-six, a very good year for blondes."

Sonny took the pills into the kitchen. He washed the dishes and dried them and put them away and then took a clean glass from the set he had bought at a discount store because Jessica had kept all the kitchen stuff when she threw him out, and filled it with water and took the two sedatives. He dried the glass and put it away and swept the kitchen floor before returning to the living room with the carton of milk he had taken from the refrigerator hours before and left on the kitchen table.

The living room was very neat. It pleased him. It had always pleased him. It was a comfortable room, a bachelor room, a room that said he entertained but lived alone. He had plumped the pillows on the couch and returned three books to the bookcase against the wall near the windows. He never let the place get worse than an hour's good cleaning would take care of. His mother had brought him up neat, and Jessica had not let him get lazy about his share of the housework. He hadn't dusted—only his mother would notice—but he had run the vacuum cleaner over the rug, the sound reminding him of the electric polisher that had been running in the hall while he waited in the outer office for his visit with Dr. Krugman this morning. The man and his daughter, whom he had seen later in the parking lot, were they home now contemplating a similar action? Had Dr. Krugman told them the same hard news?

"Was that only this morning?"

The nurse, a brunette with good legs and a high, pert bosom, had gotten up from behind her desk and opened the door to Dr. Krugman's inner office for him —was this a courtesy she reserved for the dying ones? —and she had tried to stop him when he left after his fifteen-minute meeting with the doctor. "Mr. Lawson, you are supposed to make another appointment!" she had called after him as he bolted down the medical center's eighth-floor hallway to the elevators. But there was no sense in that. No sense at all.

His fingers were sorting the pills again, the capsules suddenly reminding him of the shiny, bright-colored rubber one of the whores had brought the night Jessica had caught him, pants down, in the living room of their house. Had he wanted Jessica to catch him? Had it been an easy way to end the marriage? The rubber had felt so smooth, just like the capsules he now used to begin a little cage, the bottom of a little pyramid. Carefully he made a square with the capsules and began fitting the pills inside, piling them up until there was a small mound on the table. Julie had had a collection of little stones that she played with for hours when she was a child. . . .

"But she's still a child. And what about the business? I'm running out on that, too."

"And better off everyone will be without me," Sonny said, realizing that he was beginning to get tired. Not groggy, just a little tired. It hadn't been his idea, Lake Crest Estates, he'd just allowed himself to be talked into it—and he had never really liked the real-estate business, anyway, had never really found anything he liked to do, except those things that pleased his body. In high school he had been a diver, and he was pretty good, too, maybe good enough to have gone on to compete in serious competitions if he'd stuck with it, but Ben had talked him into switching to baseball, which he also played but didn't like as much, because his marks weren't good, and it was easier to get a baseball scholarship than one in swimming and diving in Boston.

He'd gotten the scholarship, but it had all been second-string from then on. He'd pitched in relief, and he had won some games, but he'd felt second-string, and he'd had to cheat his way through to fulfill his language and history requirements. Clever enough not to get caught, Sonny thought. That's what I was, that's what

I've always been, and that's what I want on my tombstone.

The idea struck him as enormously funny, and he laughed a great belly laugh, and picked the pile of pills up in his hands, and dribbled them through his fingers onto the glass tabletop, watching them bounce. They made little *ping*-ing noises. Several rolled off the table, and he carefully retrieved them and counted again. One was missing. He looked for it under the couch, getting down on his hands and knees and lifting the dust ruffle. He couldn't find it. He was down to fifty-five. It was okay. Fifty-five was a lot easier. Five rows of eleven. Eleven rows of five. It was plenty.

"Furthermore . . ."

If he took one more, he could have nine rows of six —six pills at a time he could swallow. He arranged the pills in nine little piles of six each, six different pills to a pile. It left him an odd capsule. He took it. How many had he taken? Three? Four? He was feeling a little sleepy, but nothing dangerous. He would have to be careful. He didn't want to simply go to sleep.

"They're all better off without me—I know they're better off without me."

He looked around his living room, ticking off those who would be better off without him by the things in the room that served as reminders. The overstuffed pillow on the floor near the hi-fi set that Mary Ellen had bought and covered for him. Yes, Mary Ellen would be better off without him, Mary Ellen of the soft calf eyes and the smooth skin and the no-orgasm-ever cunt between her legs. She'd be better off without him. The leather ottoman he'd taken from the house when Jessica threw him out. Jessica, Jessica, who hadn't been strong enough to keep him from making his first risky real-estate deal, the one that had pushed John Ashton into bankruptcy, John, who had brought him to California in the first place, who had told Sonny that he was going to drive his car over a cliff, and Sonny had laughed and told him not to worry, and he'd driven his car off the cliff.

"This is the coward's way out, that's why I picked it," Sonny said, breaking the pills out of their pattern and arranging them in three piles of eighteen. He could gulp them down one, maybe two piles at a time, with just a couple of slugs of milk.

And then there were the lamps on the end tables, pale ceramic green with gold flecks, lamps he had loved as a child and insisted on taking when his parents sold the house. His parents. They would be better off without him. His father wouldn't worry anymore that something could go wrong; his mother would have another excuse to watch television.

And the blasted stuffed three-foot-long crocodile that Marty had given him when he first started dating Mary Ellen, yes, Marty would miss him, and maybe he wouldn't be better off, but he'd find someone else to share enchilada lunches with. . . .

Sonny crossed to his desk and pulled a thin sheaf of papers from a cubbyhole. He was definitely feeling sleepy, and he couldn't leave his friends—Jessica—Julie—oh, Julie—with unnecessary work. He quickly wrote checks to pay his back bills, glad that his hands weren't shaking, glad that there was at least a few hundred dollars left. He wrote a check to Jessica for nearly the entire balance, because she'd need it for Julie until the insurance money came through, then sealed the envelopes and stamped them and put then in the mailbox outside his apartment door. The air smelled fresh and sweet. Dusk had fallen, and he looked at his watch. Where had the day gone? Where was it going?

He had a sudden fleeting pang for six oysters on the half shell and an end cut from a standing prime rib roast, and just as suddenly the pain in his stomach was there, a six, no, a seven—an eight! The worst pain he had ever had, and he doubled over to keep himself from falling, and with the aid of a hand on the straight-back chair, and then the wicker rocker, he made his way back to the couch and collapsed full length before drawing himself into a fetal position.

"I could call the suicide-prevention hot line."

The pills were on the table right in front of him, three piles now, and he could just scoop a pile up and the milk was right there to wash them down, and if he didn't hurry he would be too sleepy to do it and he'd wake up in the morning with a downer headache and the pain would be back and next time it would be a nine.

"I'd get a taped voice saying, 'Sorry, you have reached a disconnected number. . . .' "

He spotted the missing pill, which had rolled across the rug and come to rest at the base of a floor lamp he'd stolen from a motel room one drunken night when he'd had a mad on for Jessica and he and Marty had picked up a couple of crazies and a bottle of Southern Comfort.

He crawled across the rug and retrieved the pill and couldn't quite swallow it without water, reaching for the milk to wash it down, and unexpectedly he found two of the piles of pills in his hand, and then they were in his mouth, and the milk carton was to his lips, and he started to swallow, and the milk was spoiled, so rancidly horrible that the milk and the pills were spewed from his mouth by a reflex so strong nothing in his power could stop it from happening.

The pills confronted him—twenty, twenty-five, maybe thirty spots on the carpet, little spits of milk in between, and it was awful, awful, and he let his fingers do the finding for him, his eyes avoiding the mess on the carpet, his face, he knew, frozen in a grimace of distaste. One, two, three at a time, he returned the pills to the top of the coffee table, wet pills now, with the rancid milk still sticking in places, and he knew he had to get the milk off.

He got a glass of water and a bowl and a roll of

paper towels from the kitchen, and it was a chore, it seemed to take so long, he was getting tired, and one by one he dunked the pills into the water and washed off the milk, throwing the pills into the bowl until all the milk-wet pills had been washed, a terrible job, and then he gave it up and dumped them all into a paper towel and mashed them around, and closed his eyes and popped the wad of pills into his mouth and washed it down with water and swallowed, and felt a lump in his throat and then the lump broke up and he knew the pills were hitting his stomach, and he was surprised to realize that he was on his knees on the floor, moaning and keening, his hands clasped before his chest in the attitude he had assumed in the confessional, but he had been wanting comfort then, and now he was seeking. . . .

"It doesn't happen immediately. It isn't going to happen all at once!"

It was a new idea, a dessert idea, a strawberry of an idea, and Sonny took the pile of dry pills as a present to himself, an after-dinner brandy, a cigar.

"I never had my own dog.

"I have not written a suicide note."

It was a milestone. The first time he'd spoken two consecutive unrelated sentences, but that fact didn't register on Sonny until he was seated at his desk, a tablet of writing paper in front of him, a black pen in his hand because this was no time to fool around with colored Pentel pens, no one wanted a pink-and-blue suicide note, and no matter who he addressed the note to, someone would be hurt, except he knew he couldn't address it to his father because his father might not read it, and his hand suddenly looked blurry, the way his hands sometimes looked blurry when they hit the water when he was diving, but that was years ago, years since he'd done that, and the pool looked so formidable from the high boards, so frightening, but not little and square like a piece of blank notepaper.

"Dear Julie, Please forgive me."

Ah, so sweet she had been when he had let her give him her love, sweet Julie, Daddy's Girl. . . .

"I left the hat in the Jaguar."

But there was no one else to write the note to, really, only Julie, and what could he tell her, anyway? His hand was moving across the paper with a will of its own, and someplace in his brain was beginning to chant, *"You are losing motor control, you are losing motor control,"* over and over like Hal's voice in *2001,* and his hand was trying, trying very hard, but he couldn't quite connect his letters, and it took him the entire width of the page to write "Dear Julie," the letters slanting to the right, looking like the letters Julie had written in the second grade.

He tore the paper from the pad and crumpled it, and tossed it in the direction of the wastepaper basket, missing the basket, pulling the chair over with him when he tried to retrieve it, but retrieve it he did, carefully dropping it in the direction of the basket and missing again, but getting it right the third time, the crucial time, the best time, the strike-him-out-in-the-bottom-of-the-ninth-with-the-bases-loaded time, the popping-of-first-virgin's-cherry-without-coming-too-fast time, the getting-the-chair-back-before-the-desk-without-falling-to-the-floor time.

"Shit."

His vision was very blurry, but he knew his writing was almost illegible, he had waited too long, the *D* in "Dear Julie" taking up half the page, the *e* looking like a basketball hoop, the *a* sliding off the right margin onto the surface of the desk, leaving the imprint of the pen point scratched into the surface of the wood itself, and the knocking at the door sounded very loud, the one, two, three heavy raps, repeating themselves, insistent, and Sonny was scared, very frightened, and he dragged himself along the floor, tipping over the floor lamp, which crashed, a lightbulb breaking, and the pounding in his ears merged with the pounding at the door, and a voice he had heard before was calling his name, "Sonny Lawson, Sonny Lawson," over and over, pounding again, guiding him, and he pulled himself up, using the doorknob for support, and opened the door, and it wasn't Saint Peter, but Brian Flannery, Officer Brian Flannery, Flannery with two *n*'s, who had a citation in his hand, just like he'd promised, and an open mouth to go with the look of confusion on his face, and Sonny had a last laugh, seeing the man on a motorcycle guiding his own funeral procession.

"Sonny Lawson . . . ," Officer Flannery started to say.

"Not anymore," Sonny said, and collapsed in a heap on the floor.

PART TWO

Prologue

MARLON BORUNKI RUBBED HIS HANDS. That bastard
Booker. He had taken away his pencil sharpener again.
Was that on Wednesday? Quickly Marlon flipped to the
calendar he had hand-drawn at the back of his notebook. No. *Pencil sharpener confiscated* was on Tuesday. Marlon pursed his lips in concentration and began
the task of hand-sharpening the pencil, chipping away
the wood with his fingernail and rubbing the pencil on
the inside lid of the notebook until it pointed enough.
For a year now he had been trying to get Dr. Kling to
listen. He—Marlon Borunki!—called a truce on pencil
sharpeners! True, he *could* suggest to one of the people
he interviewed that a pencil sharpener smashed with a
shoe would yield a blade which could be pressed into
service, but he had given his word! There was no reason to take away his pencil sharpener. Dr. Kling had
seen parts of his manuscript. Surely he realized the importance—the *importance*—of the work. Original thinking and statistics—that should count for something.
That should count for something.

"Shouldn't that count for something?" he asked himself, turning his head. "Yes, that should count for something," he answered.

Lovingly Marlon turned the pages of his notebook,
stopping one turn short of exposing the statistics page.
He had not had a single success, and his self-imposed
limit approached. Just one more chance. Ninety-nine
chances he had had. Ninety-nine responses to his ques-

tionnaires, and ninety-nine observations, and ninety-nine failures, because eighty-eight had left La Playa, and eleven were still in the cottage. He had not helped a single suicide carry out their deed.

But it was going to be soon, now. He had felt it for hours, no, more nearly for a day. This morning. Before dawn. Marlon was sure of it. Hadn't Stillerton been making bird noises all night in the room next door? That happened in seventy-nine percent of the cases. Hadn't a car arrived earlier, and hadn't Dr. Kling walked out to greet the visitors, two adults? That happened in eighty-three percent of the cases. And hadn't Dr. Kling stopped momentarily in the driveway to look up toward his—Marlon Borunki's!—window? A surreptitious glance, to be sure, but a glance nevertheless. After number fifteen, that had happened in ninety-seven percent of the night admissions. Why, even with the first fifteen added in, that amounted to. . . .

Marlon hurried to the window. The squeak of the main gates opening had cut through the night. Soft-white spotlights flooded the grounds. Between the Administration Building and the three dormitory-style buildings that housed the inmates could be seen beds of the flowers, patches of trees and bushes, and beyond, toward the fence, a beautiful Japanese-style footbridge that led over a quarter-acre pond to a parklike area beyond; night shadows made the scene eerie, although even in the artificial light it was obvious that the grounds were beautifully kept.

A private ambulance was gliding quietly around the circular drive, pulling up before the main building. The new guard, Will Eames, was walking toward the ambulance from the direction of Middle Cottage, and Dr. Trunsand, the night-duty man, was coming from the building. Marlon turned off his desk lamp and removed the towel which he had used to shade it further. He ran the towel, warm from the heat of the bulb, over his face before returning to the window. It had to be. It had to be.

"It's got to be," he said to himself, and slapped his hand for his impatience. That was rule number one, to remain calm during waiting, but it had been a simple infraction, and simple infractions got punished with a hand slap.

Now Dr. Kling and the visitors were joining the scene. Dr. Trunsand was standing on the far side of the ambulance, talking to the driver. Will Eames was standing a few steps behind him, and then Marlon's heart lurched. Dr. Trunsand had turned to talk to Will Eames, and he had pointed to Middle Cottage. So it wasn't his night after all. It was a nervous breakdown, not a suicide. Marlon could feel his hands clenching the windowsill, bracing for the rage that was about to come. . . . Was Will Eames shaking his head? It wasn't really quite so easy to see. Yes, he had definitely shaken his head, and he was pointing to White Cottage. It was White Cottage after all! And then Dr. Kling and the visitors—a man in a suit and a woman in a white dress and high heels—were cutting across the lawn, and the ambulance was moving slowly down the path, Will Eames walking at its side, and Marlon watched them stop and open the back door, and one of the night-duty men had come out to help with the stretcher. The woman was crying and turned to be comforted by her companion.

When he first began his watches, it had mattered desperately to Marlon that the ambulances stopped in front of White Cottage in a way that often prevented him from seeing if the patients who got carried in on stretchers were male or female. The attendants carried the stretchers from the back. Sometimes, if the angle of the ambulance was just so, he would get a good view, but most of the time—eighty-five percent of the time—when the ambulances arrived at night he couldn't see.

But it no longer bothered him.

93

In fact, he rather liked it.

He thought of it as a surprise, like the sex of a new-born baby to a father.

Ahh, Marlon exhaled, exercising his upper lip by pushing it out as far as he could beyond his teeth, then pulling it back as far as he could in the direction of his nose. Soon it would be time to get his hundredth interview begun. He had one last idea, one very good new idea. It was going to work. He just knew it! It was probably five in the morning. The visitors had come at perhaps two. That meant the admission had probably come from County. Still asleep. What day was it? Tuesday? Wednesday? He checked the calendar in the back of his notebook. Thursday! How very neat. His first interview had been on a Thursday, and his fiftieth as well. Eleven percent were on Thursday.

There was really no hurry. They rarely woke while it was still dark out if they came from County in the middle of the night. Less than five percent.

Marlon left the window and checked the contents of his closet. It was the same as it had been last week, when the redheaded lady with the crossed eyes, number ninety-nine, had arrived. His checked jacket, and his short-sleeved striped shirt, and his bow tie. No pants, no belts, no shoes. His robe. His spare slippers. His checked jacket it would be, then. Ninety-nine had been the worst. Totally without gumption.

Marlon washed his face and brushed his teeth; it was part of the routine, and he performed the chores mechanically. He ran a brush through his bushy hair, and put on the shirt and jacket over his hospital gown, adjusting his clip-on bow tie and checking himself in the imaginary mirror that occupied the space between the nearly empty dresser and the door.

His preparations finished, Marlon returned to his bed and climbed in, pulling the sheet and light blanket over his head, closing his eyes and letting the kaleidoscope patterns slide in from the left. They were pink and green tonight and seemed to provide a map—yes, he would take the back route, behind the graveled flower bed, and enter the side entrance to White Cottage. Thursday was laundry day for White Cottage, and the side entrance door was opened at six and left open until seven. At six-thirty the desk attendant began rounds. The new admission would be put into room four. It was the only empty room in White Cottage. There were never more than twelve in White. At six forty-five Will Eames would return from his patrol and head for his morning coffee in the reception building. He—Marlon Borunki! —would hide in the clump of bushes on the west side of the cottage and make his run for the safety of the utility shed when Eames crossed the footbridge and cut across the lawn. For four and a half seconds his view of the terrain between Stenton Cottage and Middle Cottage would be blocked. And once Eames rounded the side of the Administration Building, Marlon wouldn't even have to crouch, just lickety-split, walk around the back of Middle Cottage.

Marlon began to sweat.

He wasn't going to think about it.

Twenty-eight percent of the time he had been spotted on the four-second dash to the laundry entrance door at White. It was the weak spot, no doubt about it, and yet he could see no alternative. Last time it had been Booker on duty, and he had hurt him—poked him on the behind and called him a Polish ham. Marlon could feel his sphincter muscle tightening, and he pinched himself on the thigh and forced himself to relax. He had violated rule number two!

But it was hard to relax, for Stillerton had called it a night, and the sound of his bird chirpings had stopped. He was quite a nice man, really, Stillerton was, Marlon thought, except that he was a certified loony and never spoke, never moved during the day, and spent all nights making bird sounds. But he was reliable—Marlon knew it was time to go. Stillerton always stopped chirping at six o'clock, when the duty changes began and the all-night lights went out.

Slowly, eyes closed, Marlon pulled the sheet and blanket down to his waist, folding it as he went. He adjusted his bow tie. He wiggled his toes, pulling the big ones back as far as they would go to help him balance on the run he would have to make. He tightened the muscles in his thighs, once, twice, three times. Then he ran his hands between his legs to feel his balls and penis, traced the ridge of hair that led upward to his navel, ran his index finger around the button, and opened his eyes.

He could hear the real birds reclaiming their territory as he sat up and felt around for his slippers.

Chapter Five

SO FAR AWAY they both seemed, so far away, and he couldn't place the other voice, the voices, and was he on a ship? Moving? Raining, pouring blurry rain, but he wasn't getting wet. Jessica crying? Marty? Sick. So sick. *Don't make me move!*

"He made a sound!"

"Yes, but he's still asleep. He'll sleep or be semi-conscious for hours probably. And he's going to be feeling very ill. I really do suggest that you let Mr. Lieberman take you home, and get some sleep. We can talk by phone in the morning."

"Let me take you home, Jessie. Dr. Kling's right. We'll come back tomorrow—this afternoon—look, I'm exhausted and so are you."

There were the sounds of people leaving then, and Sonny could hear them, hear them clearly, a dream, a dream so real he must remember to write it down in the morning, but that was long ago, and far away, in another dream, another voice in a different white house, telling him. . . .

With an enormous effort of will, Sonny forced himself to open his eyes and struggle up on an elbow. The room spun crazily, as if he'd had four margaritas with Marty at lunch, and his stomach was beginning to crank itself up to turn cartwheels. He was lying in a bed, facing a white wall. He didn't know where he was.

"Shit!" he murmured. "Goddammit! Sonofabitch!"

Memory began to flood back, and he inhaled an enormous breath of air, because it was. . . .

"It's interesting how you woke up cursing."

No. He didn't recognize the voice. Had never heard it before. Slowly Sonny relaxed on the bed and turned over. There was a second bed in the room, and on it was sitting a fat, bookish-looking man in his thirties, with large round eyes and a rubbery face. He was holding a good-sized notebook and a pencil stub.

"A large percentage of attempted suicides come out of their comas with exclamations of hostility," the man continued once he was certain he had Sonny's attention.

Sonny looked around the room. He was having trouble focusing. Where was he? There were bars on the window. The beds were mechanical, but there were no oxygen tanks or outlets, he was wearing comfortable striped pajamas instead of a hospital gown, there were floral curtains on the windows, and the dresser was painted red.

"Where am I?" Sonny asked.

The man on the bed looked at him with approval and chuckled with appreciation. He made a quick calculation in his notebook.

"Ninety-two percent of them ask that," he said.

The man continued to look at Sonny intently, but he seemed disinclined to talk further, and Sonny rubbed his eyes and flopped back on the pillow, turning his head so that he could watch his visitor. The man had begun flipping back and forth between two pages of his notebook, as if comparing figures.

"You're in La Playa," he said when he realized Sonny was watching him. The words got Sonny sitting up.

"The nuthouse?"

"That's a cruel label," the man said. "We prefer 'booby hatch.' "

"Are you a doctor?"

"No, no, I'm a patient," the man said, standing up

98

and sticking out a hand for Sonny to shake. Sonny responded slowly. The man was wearing a jacket and tie over a hospital nightgown.

"Marlon Borunki," the man said. "Paranoid schizophrenic, deep feelings of inferiority alternating with delusions of grandeur."

"Sonny Lawson," Sonny said. "Real estate."

Marlon was looking at him closely, slowly sticking out his bottom lip and then drawing it back in. Sonny closed his eyes. . . . Oh, God, it hadn't worked. He was still alive, and he was still dying, and he was in La Playa! The nuthatch!

"Say," Marlon was saying, "didn't you used to be on television selling land somewhere?"

No, Sonny thought, this can't be happening. It was a nightmare. It was. . . .

"Lake Crest Estates!" Marlon shrieked, raising his voice, then clapping his hand over his mouth, his eyes becoming even rounder than before. "Lake Crest Estates! You were selling parcels of land at Lake Crest Estates!" Marlon was fighting with himself for control of his hand.

"I swear there was a lake there," Sonny said, unexpectedly near to tears, and afraid, afraid of this man, and sick, feeling so sick. "I don't know where the hell it went." He had to get hold of himself! He shut his eyes and got his swimming vision under control, and forced his stomach to behave. Maybe he was dreaming after all, and he could open his eyes, and. . . .

Marlon Borunki was still there. He had retreated to sit on the edge of the other bed again, and he was watching Sonny with a benevolent look in his eyes.

"You didn't buy a lot there, did you?" Sonny asked, knowing that Marlon hadn't, and that he was safe, but needing to know, anyway.

"Oh, no," Marlon confirmed. "I don't buy land on TV. I'm crazy, but I'm not that crazy." His eyes began a detailed inspection of Sonny, beginning at the foot of the bed and moving slowly upward. His expression became one of admiration.

"Gee, a real TV star," he said. "Only one percent of my subjects have been real TV stars."

"How'd I get in here?" Sonny asked.

"They transferred you last night from County."

"How do you know that?"

"I overheard them."

"Who?" Sonny asked.

"Dr. Kling and the man and woman."

"What man and woman?" Sonny asked.

"Mrs. Lawson and Mr. Lieberman," Marlon said. "They signed you in. You tried to kill yourself. Unsuccessfully, I might add. Then why did you do it, dummy?"

Sonny closed his eyes again when Marlon bit himself on the shoulder—probably as punishment for his last remark—and then kissed the spot. He wanted to burrow into the bed. Anything to make the dizziness go away. There must be something that could be done for the nausea. Marlon would know. Marlon was part of the problem. Go away, Sonny willed. Leave me alone and let me die!

But Marlon was still sitting on the opposite bed, watching him minutely. Waiting, it seemed, to demand Sonny's entire attention. He was holding up his manuscript book.

"I'm writing a book on insanity. I call it *A View from the Other Side.*" With a gesture of pride Marlon riffled the pages of the notebook in Sonny's direction. "I've got two whole chapters on suicide, and when I finish with my statistics chart, the book will be finished."

"That's very nice, Marlon," Sonny said. He wondered if he could cut his wrists with a piece of Marlon's notepaper. Writers got paper cuts all the time, didn't they?

"Did you know that almost fifty percent of all female suicides have bleached hair and a hysterectomy scar?"

Sonny wanted to scream, but he seemed to have forgotten how to do it. He tore his eyes away from Marlon's face and stared at the ceiling. He had needs of his own, could summon no approval for this man and his enthusiasm. Were the walls plaster? Could he chip away and swallow pieces? . . . Marlon's sympathetic face appeared in his line of vision; he had come to stand by Sonny's bed.

"Are you depressed?" Marlon asked suddenly.

"Yeah," Sonny said. "I'm depressed." It was as good a definition of how he was feeling as any.

"Why?" Marlon said. "It's important to know why."

"I thought I'd wake up dead," Sonny said, and the thought of Jessica and Marty bringing him here to this place flooded him with a surge of energy in the form of anger. "They had no right to barge in and stop me!" he said. He was having trouble with his tongue, the words sounding slow and slurred.

Marlon made a noise of commiseration with his lips. "Technically, they have a right," he said. "It's against the law to kill yourself."

"You're kidding," Sonny said. He shook his head. The movement brought pain, but cleared a few cobwebs.

"No," Marlon said. He retreated to the open bed, flipped open his book, and held it up for Sonny to catch a glance. "The laws vary from state to state, but suicide is legislated against in most of them. It's all here, in the appendix of my book."

"That's the dumbest thing I ever heard of," Sonny said.

Marlon had removed his right slipper and seemed to be exercising his toes. "I agree with you," he said. "It's always struck me that it is just as presumptuous to tell a person how to die as it is to tell them how to live."

"What a dumb law," Sonny said, shaking his head again as a test. It hurt less than the last time, but the pain in his stomach . . . oh, God, his stomach! The doctor . . . he was dying!

"Sane people make a lot of crazy rules," Marlon said.

There was silence in the room then, and Sonny realized that it was daylight. How long had he been asleep? What had happened? Julie. He had been thinking about Julie, wanting to write her a note, and then a sledgehammer had started at the door . . . no, it had just been knocking . . . the policeman from the funeral cortege. . . .

"Do you like me?" Marlon said unexpectedly, carefully putting his notebook on the bed, slipping the pencil into the wire spiral that held the pages together.

"Sure, Marlon," Sonny said. "I don't know you very well, but—"

"Oh, you know all there is to know. I'm very superficial. I know it, and I said it, and I won't argue with myself about it." Marlon smiled at Sonny apologetically. "I just committed a misdemeanor," he explained, unexpectedly snarling and biting the back of his hand. "I broke my third rule, which I cannot divulge."

Sonny took a deep breath and began to test his arms and legs for strength. He was going to have to get out of here. Could he do anything with the wire in Marlon's notebook?

"Marlon, do you share this room with me?"

"Oh, no," Marlon said. "I'm in the South Wing. That's where the real dangerous ones are kept."

"Are you dangerous?"

"Well, my father thought I was."

"And he put you in here?" Sonny asked, not quite sure he was following the story.

"Oh, no," Marlon said. "I strangled him. I guess he was right. Every doctor has a different theory why I did it—father complex, feeling of rejection, suppressed rage. But I know the real reason. It was because he was so Polish."

"Polish?" Sonny suppressed an impulse to giggle.

Marlon nodded. "Ever since I was a little child I've been taunted by Polish jokes. You don't understand, do you?"

Sonny shook his head. He was feeling sick again, and he had to urinate.

"What's your name?" Marlon demanded.

"Sonny. Sonny Lawson. I told you that before. You even wrote it in your book."

"Yes, that's right." Marlon said. "You're number one hundred, you know."

"Number one hundred what?"

"Number one hundred attempted suicides who I've interviewed since I've been at La Playa. Suicides are seventy-eight percent less likely to tell me Polish jokes than anyone else I've encountered."

"I don't understand," Sonny said. His voice sounded strange in his ears. Who was this man? What was he doing here?

"You don't understand?" Marlon said. "You don't understand about Polish jokes? You know, 'How can you tell a Polack's identification? By the shit in his wallet.' Or, 'Who was Poland's Man of the Year? Nobody.' Or, 'How do you sing the Polish National Anthem? You don't sing it, you fart it.'"

Sonny shook his head. "Kids are cruel," he said. Why had he said that?

"What kids?" Marlon said. "These were told to me by my father. He teased me all the time. The big, loud, hairy, sweaty Polack!" Marlon was getting visibly excited; sweat had formed on his upper lip, which he had extended out over his teeth in a grimace that reminded Sonny of a monkey in a zoo. "He was always covered with sweat," Marlon said, raising his voice and wiping his upper lip with an index finger. "He's the only person I know who sweated while he was swimming."

Sonny looked at Marlon and raised his hands in supplication. How could he possibly respond to this tirade?

"And stupid!" Marlon continued. "He thought Moby Dick was a venereal disease. I could never have friends over. He'd challenge them to nose-picking contests."

Marlon had stopped watching Sonny, and was now staring at a spot on the wall above his head, midway between the floor and the ceiling. He was trembling and shaking, and his face was contorting, changing expression with every sentence.

"The last straw was the night I finally brought a girl home." Marlon was saying. "I knew I shouldn't have done it. There he was, sitting in his favorite sweaty undershirt, drinking beer and watching 'Celebrity Bowling' . . . eating chili with his fingers."

Sonny pinched himself on the thigh, under the sheet. He could feel it. So this wasn't a dream, it really was happening.

"At first he was nice," Marlon said, his expression doleful. He grabbed the sheet on the bed with both hands. "Then, just as the young lady and I were leaving for dinner, he told her that she shouldn't waste an evening with a loser like me."

Sonny watched as Marlon's hands tightened on the sheet. They were steady, but the rest of his body had begun to tremble.

"I put my hands around his twenty-two-inch neck and strangled him!" Quickly Marlon turned his head to the left. "You say it like you're proud!" he said in a high, squeaky voice, immediately turning his head to the right and adding, "Well, you didn't have the guts to do it."

Marlon's trembling stopped, and he reached for his

notebook again, smiling at Sonny as if he'd been talk-ing about the weather or an interesting game of golf.

"Oh, God, I'm sick," Sonny said.

"After I was born, Mother left me and my father," Marlon continued. "I always respected her for that. And I wonder, do you think this country will ever have the sense to switch over to the metric system? I wish they would."

"I wish I was dead," Sonny said, meaning every word of it. "And I have to go to the bathroom."

Marlon nodded his approval. "One hundred percent of all new arrivals have to go to the bathroom."

With an effort of will, Sonny raised himself up to a sitting position, pulled off the sheet, and tried to swing his legs to the floor. He was woozy, and his arms and legs felt rubbery, as if the connections between his brain and his muscles had been short-circuited.

"You shouldn't get up yet," Marlon said, reaching under the bed and offering Sonny a stainless-steel bed-pan.

Sonny shook his head. "I can't pee into that," he said.

By turning on his side and using his arms, Sonny managed to maneuver his legs to the side of the bed; he let them dangle over. When he sat up again, he could feel them tentatively tapping the floor. It was very cold, surprisingly cold, and he knew that his balance was precarious, that he was wavering. He turned so that he was half facing the bed, and using his arms for leverage and support, finally got himself on his feet. For a moment or two he could not stand without using his arms, nearly falling during the single step he took to reach the foot of the bed.

"I'll get a nurse," Marlon said.

"No," Sonny said quickly. "I can't pee with a nurse around."

Slowly, exercising great care, Sonny edged along the foot of the bed and negotiated the few feet to the bathroom, remembering that the last time he had been on his feet he had also had to use the furniture to help him; and then he was in the white-tiled bathroom, leaning against the wall next to the toilet, and it wasn't Officer Flannery at the door. . . .

"Please, Marlon," Sonny said, not wanting to antagonize the crazy man. "I can't pee with the door open." Gently Sonny closed the door.

"You've got a lot of rules about peeing," Marlon shouted through the door, as if it were made of concrete instead of wood.

"Yeah?" Sonny said, a vision of Marlon's elastic face staying with him behind the retinas of his eyes. He reached down to lift the toilet seat, but the movement made him dizzy, and with a sigh of resignation and defeat, he sat, like a boy. He ran his hands over his face. Stubble. He ran his hands over his arms; strength was returning to his arms. He directed his urine, flushed, managed to stand, closed the toilet top, and sat again. The cloth of the pajama top was very strong. His legs wouldn't hold him. If he could . . .

He wasn't going to go through this. Nurses changing his diapers . . . He felt the material of his pajama top again. His arms were feeling stronger now. If he could secure the top to the light fixture in the ceiling . . .

"Mr. Lawson?" There was a timid knock from Marlon at the door.

How was he going to do it? Sonny shrugged out of the pajama top and examined it. If he used one sleeve to tie to the light fixture . . . but with one sleeve occupied, how could he knot the other one. . . .

Marlon had opened the door and was watching him.

"I don't think it will work. Do you?" Sonny asked.

"Uh-uh," Marlon said, shaking his head; his cheeks seemed to settle down at a pace of their own.

Marlon offered his arm, and with his help Sonny

got to his feet. There was no medicine chest in the bathroom, and nothing that looked the least bit helpful in the other room. Sonny took a couple of steps, then removed his hand from Marlon's and managed to stand in the center of the room, between the beds, without support.

"Damn," he said. "Isn't there anything around here a guy can kill himself with?"

"They're pretty thorough," Marlon said, a strange look resembling hope on his face. "No razors, no glasses, no mirrors."

"No mirrors?" Sonny felt his face. The stubble felt as if it had already grown. "They can't do this to me!" Without thinking, he inhaled an enormous breath of air, puffing out his cheeks.

Marlon watched him for a few seconds, then sat on the edge of the bed again and reached for his notebook.

"You're holding your breath, hoping to suffocate," he said.

Sonny nodded. Yes, that's what he was doing!

"It won't work," Marlon said. "It's been tried by" —he consulted his notebook—"sixteen percent. Once you pass out, you start breathing again. You'll just get a headache."

Sonny blew out the air in disgust and watched Marlon as he began to fiddle with the up-and-down button on the electric bed. All the way up, all the way down, and then Marlon was looking at him with that peculiar glint in his eyes.

"I wonder if you could stick your head in there and crack it. Sort of like a walnut." He pushed the control button again, watching Sonny closely. "Ahh, it's a crazy idea," he said.

"Sometimes those are the best kind," Sonny said, taking a good look at Marlon and then groping to the bed to examine the controls and the mechanism. Maybe, just maybe . . .

Marlon had reached for his hand, obviously upset; there were footsteps in the hallway.

"It's Carl!" Marlon said. "And Booker!"

And then the door opened and two men dressed in white uniforms entered the room. One of them was a tall black man, and the other, white, was short but stocky and muscular. He reminded Sonny of a dwarf.

Marlon had left the bed and was retreating slowly toward a corner of the room, and the black attendant was following him slowly, holding out a straitjacket and taunting him.

"Tsk-tsk, Marlon, you've been making up your own visiting hours again," he said.

"Leave me alone, Carl," Marlon whined.

"You're to come with me, Mr. Lawson," the short, stocky man said. "My name is Booker."

Sonny instinctively backed away, his legs feeling slightly less wobbly.

"Get away from me with that thing," Marlon was saying.

"Just think of it as a Polish dinner jacket," Carl said. Booker laughed.

"How can you make fun about a problem that's not his fault and that he's obviously sensitive about?" Sonny said, furious with the men, furious with his situation.

Booker and Carl exchanged glances, not used to having Marlon defended.

"We're sorry," Booker said, gently taking Sonny by the arm. "Now, please, come with me. Dr. Kling wants to see you."

Carl had gotten hold of Marlon now and was fastening him in the straitjacket, and Sonny pulled away from Booker to try to help him, but Booker was very strong and easily restrained him. Sonny pushed again, futilely—God, he was so weak! "Get your hands off me, you little dwarf!" he yelled, but Booker just laughed and easily pushed Sonny out of the room.

"I escape with great frequency, Mr. Lawson," Marlon said.

"Sonny," Sonny said, as Booker pushed him out the door.

"Okay, Sonny," Marlon said. "Hey, Carl, that's my friend Sonny."

Some friend, Sonny thought as he ran out of energy to resist and let Booker lead him down the hall, concentrating on making his legs and feet function. Booker held tightly to his arm, but both men knew it was really an unnecessary precaution. There was no way Sonny could make his body function enough to escape. A resentment more intense than he had ever experienced flooded Sonny as Booker led him to the Administration Building, to a door marked HEAD OF PSYCHIATRY. He opened the door without waiting for a reply to his knock.

It was a cheerful office, with plants everywhere, on every surface, and hanging in baskets from the windows. A man in his late fifties was seated behind an orderly desk. He was thin and wiry, with wide-set eyes and a narrow nose. His hair was dark. He gave an impression of nervousness as he rose and motioned Booker to let Sonny's arm go.

At the first sign of release Sonny pulled himself away from Booker, who looked at Dr. Kling for instructions.

"You can go, Booker," Dr. Kling said, waiting beside his desk until Booker had left the room. Sonny felt ludicrous dressed in pajama bottoms with the top tied around his neck. But Dr. Kling didn't seem to notice that, and now he offered his hand.

"Mr. Lawson, I'm Dr. Kling." Dr. Kling waited for a few seconds, and when Sonny did not return his gesture of friendship he returned to sit behind the desk, motioning Sonny to sit in either of the two chairs that faced it. Sonny had the sudden absurd notion that it was a test, and deliberately continued to stand, although he wanted desperately to sit, to be alone, in control of his life again, perhaps at Mary Ellen's, where he could wait and find the gun. . . .

"How are you feeling?"

"Cheated," Sonny said as quickly as if he had been responding to a Rorschach test. "Is it true that Jessica and Marty checked me in?"

"Yes. You were rushed to County Hospital last night. Your stomach was pumped. Jessica Lawson was notified, and she and Martin Lieberman made the decision to have you transferred here. Do you remember any of this? You were semiconscious at one point, I think."

"Don't start asking me questions," Sonny said. He was feeling very hostile. "Just tell me how I get out of here."

"Well, a lot depends on you," Dr. Kling said.

"What does that mean?" Sonny said, knowing what that meant, walking over to the desk and sitting in the larger chair.

"It means your release depends a great deal on your mental state," Dr. Kling said. He was toying with a blunt plastic letter opener, the sight of which annoyed Sonny tremendously. He wondered if the doctor kept a pair of children's scissors in his desk.

"Here is my mental state," Sonny said carefully. *"I want out."* He took care to pronounce the words distinctly and calmly, looking at Dr. Kling's face, wishing that he were dressed, wishing that he were not involved in this hideous conversation.

"Mr. Lawson, I think you know what I'm trying to say," Dr. Kling said, watching his fingers and occasionally glancing up quickly, as if hoping to catch Sonny in an incriminating action. "We can't let you out of here until we're sure you're not going to destroy yourself."

"It's none of your goddamn business if I want to

destroy myself!" Sonny yelled, losing control, pounding his fist on the desk with frustration.

"Perhaps I could help you find out why you want to do it," Dr. Kling said, looking Sonny square in the face, daring him to turn away.

"I know why!" Sonny said. "It's very simple. I've got a job that makes me vomit, an ex-wife and kid that keep me dripping with guilt. I'm in love with a twelve-year-old who won't come, and I've got an incurable disease that is going to cause me to shit all over myself while I die a painful death!"

"That sounds a lot like self-pity," Dr. Kling said piously.

"It *is* self-pity. And so what if it's self-pity? It's true. Now let me out of here so I can do something about it!" And the pain struck then, an eight, a nine . . . his first ten! . . . and it was so horrible that he doubled over, falling from the chair. The chair went over, too, and he knew that Dr. Kling had gotten up and was coming around the side of the desk; and he tried to stand, tried to unbend, but there was no strength, no strength at all in his legs, and he knew that he was blacking out. He fought to retain consciousness, fought as Booker and Dr. Kling supported him between them on the interminable walk back to his room, fought to say hello when Jessica's voice unexpectedly came ripping into his awareness.

"Dr. Kling, what's the matter with him?"

"He tried to get up too soon, Mrs. Lawson," Dr. Kling said. "Now please, let us get him back to his room before we talk."

He must have passed out for a few minutes then, because he awoke in a daze, back in bed, and it was Marty's hand he felt on his shoulder. Sonny turned his face to the wall. "Go away, you traitor," he said.

"Mrs. Lawson, Mr. Lieberman, would you care to join me for a few minutes in the hall?" Dr. Kling was saying.

Sonny thought he heard Jessica crying, but he was nauseous again, and possessed with an exhaustion so terrible that he could not fathom it.

"Come on, Jessie," Marty was saying, his voice distant but distinct. "Pull yourself together. That isn't going to do Sonny any good. He's going to be okay."

"He's going to die in three months, that's what Mary Ellen said," Jessica said.

"No, he's not going to die in three months," Dr. Kling's voice said, louder than Jessica's or Marty's. Sonny had a hunch that the doctor was holding the conversation outside his door deliberately, that he was meant to overhear it, but there wasn't anything he could do about it, anyway.

"What do you mean?" Jessica said.

"I spoke with Dr. Krugman this morning after Mr. Lawson was transferred here. He's the hematologist Mr. Lawson saw yesterday morning. Dr. Krugman's opinion—a very good one indeed, by the way—is that Mr. Lawson has a year and perhaps even eighteen months to live. Mr. Lawson pressed Dr. Krugman until he admitted that in some unusual cases the time involved before death could be as little as three months, and apparently Mr. Lawson simply didn't listen beyond that point in Dr. Krugman's statement."

"A year," Marty said. "Listen, Jessica, he's got at least a year."

"It doesn't matter," Jessica said. "He's not going to believe you. He heard three months, and he believes three months, and I just know he'll try it again. Sonny likes to get his way."

That's exactly right, Sonny thought. I don't believe it. He didn't believe it at all. And it didn't matter, anyway. Six months of pain, a year of pain, what difference did it make? He wanted out now, *now*, before it came again, before he had another ten. He was so tired, felt so dreadful, please!

"And besides, he's very resourceful." It was Jessica

talking again. "If he's made up his mind to . . . to commit suicide . . . he's going to try it again."

"Set your mind at ease, Mrs. Lawson," Dr. Kling said. "There's no way he can hurt himself in here."

Except with the help of Marlon Borunki, Sonny thought, realizing that he was about to lose consciousness again. Except with the help of Marlon Borunki . . .

Chapter Six

IT WAS EARLY EVENING when Sonny woke into a dream-like place, a state of mind that reminded him of the films of Antonioni. Someone had come into the room and turned on a soft overhead light, although perhaps the lights were controlled from a central switch. He remembered that a male attendant had come in earlier with a tray of food, but Sonny had gagged at the odor and waved him away. Even earlier a nurse had come and taken his pulse, and twice—no, three times—the door had opened and people had come to stand beside his bed. Once he had gotten the whiff of perfume? A nurse? Jessica again? He hadn't opened his eyes. Would they let Julie come to see him? Mary Ellen? Could he talk Mary Ellen into bringing him the gun?

La Playa. He was in La Playa. And he had taken all those pills and it hadn't worked, and they were going to keep him here, and he couldn't bear it. He couldn't bear it!

The dizziness seemed to have passed. He had a headache. It was no effort at all to open his eyes. His pajama top was on correctly. There was water in a plastic glass on the night table next to his bed. He must have been tossing restlessly, because the sheet had nearly pulled free at the bottom of the bed— quite a feat, he knew, for a bed made with hospital corners. He could see the gap between the mattress and the metal frame of the bed, where the mechanism for the mattress was housed. He fumbled around and found the control box, which was pinned to the sheet beside the left side of his pillow. Tentatively Sonny pushed the button. Automatically the bed responded by raising the head of the mattress. Sonny held the button down until the top of the mattress forced him to sit up straight and then begin to bend forward. Slowly he reversed the mechanism. He lay flat on his back for quite a while. Yes, it might work. It just might work. If he could figure out a way so he could jam the button and leave it out of reach so that he couldn't stop himself. . . .

He swung his feet over the side of the bed and fished for the slippers with his toes. He was weak, still weak, but it was partially from lack of food now, because his muscles were responding, and he made it to the bathroom without having to support himself along the way. He was able to stand before the toilet without holding on as well, and he took the time to look out the window at the grounds of La Playa before returning to the bed. The grounds were lit by floodlights; a fence with barbed wire attached to the top completely surrounded the grounds. There was certainly a man on duty at the guardhouse near the entrance gates. He wondered if the fence was electrified, if he had the courage to simply walk into it. But if it was, the voltage would be set to stun, not kill. He didn't need that. He wanted no more failures. Gingerly Sonny ran his hand over his side and stomach. The area was tender, and although he was not actually in pain, he certainly was not feeling comfortable. He would never feel comfortable again. He was a victim, betrayed by his body, betrayed by his friends, betrayed by everyone but Marlon Borunki.

He crossed to the door and carefully tested the

knob. It turned silently in his hand. It wasn't locked. The door pulled open inward, and cautiously Sonny risked a glance into the hall. Where was he going to go? He didn't know. At the far end of the hall was a small cubicle, and near the cubicle was a reception area with half a dozen chairs arranged in a semicircle around a table that held magazines and ashtrays. If the chairs had been empty, it would have been an easy matter to slip out, Sonny realized, but the chairs weren't empty. Marty and Jessica were there, their backs toward his room, and silently Sonny closed the door, leaning against it in despair. What was he going to do? What was he going to do? It had been hours since the last pain, and it was going to come again, come soon, and he couldn't tolerate it, wouldn't tolerate it!

He picked up the plastic glass from the night table and gulped the water down, feeding a sudden demand from his stomach for something, anything, to soothe the pangs of emptiness. But the water didn't help at all, except to placate his dry, cottony-feeling mouth. The glass was quite light when empty, not nearly heavy enough, was it? For the fun of it, Sonny put the glass on the control button that operated the bed's mechanism. No, it wasn't heavy enough, but with a slight pressure. . . .

Sonny took the glass into the bathroom and filled it with water. He unpinned the control button from the sheet and placed it flat on the night table. Gingerly he placed the filled glass on the control device. No, still not heavy enough. What was there? What was there in the room? Nothing. There was nothing. Nothing in the closet, not even an empty hanger, and nothing in the drawers of the dresser or the night table, either. A pillow? Would a pillow work? No.

And then he spotted the notebook, Marlon Borunki's notebook, which the crazy man had obviously attempted to hide beneath the pillow of the spare bed

116

when Carl and Booker had come for them. Carefully Sonny withdrew it from its hiding place, holding it tenderly, and with infinite care he adjusted the plastic water glass on the button that would operate the bed, and carefully he lowered the book to balance on the glass. He got it right on the first try, and stood for a moment watching as the bed responded to the pressure on the button.

Kneeling then at the foot of the bed, holding onto the metal rail to support himself, Sonny placed his head at the foot of the bed, his eyes closed, knowing that there was going to be pain, a moment or two where he would be able to release himself, hoping he had the courage to survive the moment, wishing that his time were already up, hoping that the footsteps coming down the hall were not heading for his room, feeling the first slight touch of the sheet on his head, and simultaneously hearing the door open and Marty's voice screaming his name.

There were running sounds, too, and then an incredible pressure in his skull as the bed mechanism jolted downward at a faster speed than before; and then the pressure was gone and his head ached, ached horribly, and Marty was standing at the open doorway, the device that Sonny had rigged with the glass and Marlon's book in his hand. Marty's face was white, and behind him Jessica was standing, a hand to her mouth, and behind her Dr. Kling was standing, and behind him several unfamiliar people, dressed in patients' garb. And then Dr. Kling pushed into the room, looking first at Sonny and then at the bed, taking the control box from Marty's hand and regarding it speculatively.

Sonny tried to get to his feet, but he did not dare take his hands away from his splitting head. The pressure! The pressure! And the sound he heard? Was that himself moaning?

Booker was in the room now, helping him to the spare bed, forcing Sonny's hands away from his face so that Dr. Kling could examine him. Sonny forced himself to relax, exhaling slowly through his mouth.

"He's going to be all right," Dr. Kling said, as if Sonny had gone deaf.

"But he's in pain," Jessica said. "Give him something for his pain!"

Sonny balked. "Don't put me to sleep," he said. "Don't put me to sleep!"

"I won't put you to sleep, Mr. Lawson," Dr. Kling said. "I'll just give you something to help get rid of your headache."

"All right," Sonny said.

The next few minutes passed in a flurry. Sonny lay on the bed with his eyes shut, conscious of the movement around him, able to move if he wanted to, but knowing that hammers would start flailing in his head the minute he tried. He made no attempt to stop Dr. Kling from administering the injection. Someone sat on the bed.

Within a matter of minutes the awareness of pain subsided and Sonny opened his eyes. Marty was standing next to the bed, looking down at him. Jessica sat on the edge of the bed, facing him.

"Are you feeling better, Sonny?" she asked.

"No," he said.

"Do you want me to ask the nurse for anything?"

"Ask her for a thirty-two automatic," Sonny said, sitting up and forcing himself to keep his face impassive, even though the movement hurt.

"Sonny, the more you talk like that, the longer you're going to be in here," Marty said.

"I'm not going to be in here at all, Marty. I want out!"

Marty glanced worriedly toward Jessica, but remained silent. He thrust his right hand into his pants pocket, and Sonny could hear the sounds of his fingers playing with change.

"You're a lawyer, Marty," Sonny said. "Didn't you hear me? I said I want out! Bribe someone."

Marty shook his head and bit the inside of his lip. "We don't have to bribe anybody," he said.

"What do you mean?"

"All we have to do is sign a release and pay the bill."

"Then why the hell aren't you doing that right now?" Sonny yelled. Jessica was playing with the chipped polish on her thumbnail, and Marty was looking toward the bathroom door, as if he, too, wanted to escape from this room.

"Well?" Sonny said. "Why aren't you doing it?"

"Because neither one of us is sure you're not going to just get out of here and go try it again," Marty said, the sentence coming out in one breath, Marty looking everywhere in the room except at Sonny.

"Marty, look at me," Sonny said. "And you, too, Jessica." He looked from one to the other. "Now I want you both to quit worrying. No more suicide attempts . . . the next time I'm succeeding!"

Marty threw up his hands in exasperation, and Jessica pounded her thighs with her hands. "Sonny, why are you taunting us?" she said, her voice pitched high with despair. "It's like you're bragging about it."

"I'm not bragging," Sonny said, reminded of his meeting with Mary Ellen and her anger at his attempt to use her. *Was* he bragging? he asked himself. "No, I'm not bragging, Jessica," he said. "It's just what I'm going to do."

"Well, damn it, neither one of us is going to sign a release until you promise not to!" Jessica said.

Sonny looked at her. Her face was set in an expression of determination. Marty was standing his ground, also.

"Okay, I promise," Sonny said.

"Bullshit," Marty said.

"I swear on my life," Sonny said.

There was dead silence in the room then, each of them locked in their thoughts. From outside came the sounds of the La Playa gate opening to admit a vehicle and then closing again. A great variety of birds seemed to be chirping in the night. There was activity, the sound of footsteps in the hall. Whatever it was that Dr. Kling had injected him with, Sonny realized, had taken the corners off, rounded him out, shifted his mood. Without understanding why, he reached out and took Jessica's hand.

She immediately covered his hand with hers, and Sonny smiled ruefully as Marty acknowledged the interchange by shifting around on his feet, obviously pleased.

"Look, Sonny," Jessica said, "right now you're suffering from depression as much as your illness. Once the depression is over—"

"The depression isn't going to be over," Sonny said, the picture of the old man on the terminal floor branded into his memory. "I'm going to shrivel up and turn yellow. You think looking like an old Jap is going to cheer me up?" He knew his voice had gotten shrill and high.

"Sonny, calm down. Please," Jessica said.

"How can I calm down?" he asked, pushing himself into an upright position and rebuffing Marty's attempt to help with the pillow. "It's like I'm trapped in some kind of nightmare," he said. "You people won't be happy until you see me alive!"

"We're doing this because we love you," Jessica said.

"That's right," Marty said.

Sonny shook his head, relieved that the movement didn't hurt. "Anybody who really loved me wouldn't want me to suffer," he said.

Jessica was looking at him unhappily.

Marty had his hands locked behind his back.

"Please!" Sonny pleaded. "I only have a couple of days left, anyway."

"That's bullshit," Marty said. "Dr. Kling checked with the hematologist you saw yesterday. You're not going to die right away."

"Why do you always have to rush everything?" Jessica said.

"Because pretty soon I'm going to be too weak to make my own decision. So weak the courts will let assholes like you make them for me." He was looking directly at Marty.

"I don't deserve that," Marty said.

"I'm sorry," Sonny said, meaning it, "but I don't deserve to die." Well, maybe he did deserve to die, but he wanted it his own way, and he could tell from the tightness that had appeared around Marty's mouth that he was not going to change his mind. Not now, at least. Not today.

"Marty, please leave us for a while, would you at least do that? I want to talk to Jessica alone."

"No," Jessica said promptly, "I—"

"Please, honey," Sonny said, taking her hand. "Please, Marty," he said to his best friend.

Marty started to protest, then nodded. "Okay. I'll wait outside. But remember, I love you, Sonny. I'd do anything for you—be your slave, get you girls—sorry, Jessie—but I . . . I just can't do this."

"I love you, too, Marty. Now get out of here."

Sonny felt a sudden elation. Jessica was weak. She was a woman. She felt sorry for him. He was going to win because she hadn't stopped Marty from leaving the room.

"Have you had to say anything to Julie?" he asked.

"No," Jessica said. "She slept next door last night, and I told her I had a date tonight."

"Good," Sonny said. And then, because she had

121

moved away toward the foot of the bed, Sonny slowly and deliberately took both her hands in his, pulling her close to him, staring deep into her eyes.

"Jessica," he said, "you have got to sign me out of here."

Jessica tried to hold his glance, but wasn't able to. "I . . . I don't want you in a place like this," she said. "But . . . I don't want you dead, either."

Gently Sonny turned Jessica's face toward him with a hand on her chin. "Jessie, you and I are two people who once loved each other, right?"

"Right," she said after a slight hesitation, as if agreeing with his statement were a dangerous concession.

"Maybe we still love each other," he said, trying for the sound of conviction in his voice.

Jessica looked at him then, hard and long, small brown lines appearing vertically between her eyes. "I don't think so," she said finally.

"I don't think so, either," Sonny admitted. "But we could fake it a little at a time like this, couldn't we?"

Jessica shook her head. "Ever since those two hookers—"

"Will you forget the hookers?" Sonny yelled, forgetting himself, furious that she still zeroed in on that single incident, forgetting all that had happened before and all that he had tried to do since. "Isn't it ever time for you to forgive and forget? I've been as loyal as I could."

Jessica exhaled a disbelieving breath through her mouth and turned on the bed to stare at the wall across from her, her head bent. She had cleaned her thumbnail of polish, and now began working on her index finger's nail. What was going to reach her? Sonny wondered. He hadn't been able to reach her for years; what made him think he could do it now? And he needed to reach her, needed to reach her desperately; she was his only hope of getting out of here. And if he didn't get out of here . . .

"I suppose now is the time to tell you," he said then, somewhat dramatically, grasping at straws. "I'm leaving you and Julie everything."

"Everything but the three thousand dollars you're leaving that little shit, Mary Ellen," Jessica spat.

"Now is no time to discuss money," Sonny said hastily. And then he was grabbing at her hands again, pleading, "Just get me out of here, Jessie. Please sign me out of here."

Jessica was shaking her head vigorously from side to side. "Sonny, I understand what you're going through, but—"

"No, you don't!" Sonny protested. "Until you've been pronounced dead, you have no idea what I'm going through!"

"All right," Jessica conceded. "But I'm *trying* to understand."

"You're doing a lousy job of it."

Jessica pulled her hands away. Her head began to move from side to side, like a motor-driven mannequin. "I can't let you kill yourself," she said. "It's a burden I'd carry the rest of my life. Letting you take your life would make my own life meaningless." And now it was Jessica who was demanding eye contact, staring at Sonny's face with unblinking eyes. "Tell me you understand," she said.

"I understand what I've always understood," Sonny said. "You're a selfish bitch!"

Jessica promptly rose from the bed and walked to the door. Sonny threw the sheet off and caught her by the arm.

"Wait!" he said, his tone softening. "You're not a selfish bitch. You're just a wife."

"Sexist ass right to the last," she said, anger making her face hard. He didn't like the expression. It frightened him.

"Oh, Jessica," Sonny said, suddenly depressed. "Don't you see that I was just trying to be nice?"

"Forget it," she said, although she softened at his words. Then she was reaching out and straightening the collar of his pajama top, the way Mary Ellen had reached out to straighten the collar of the kimono. "We've forgotten how to be nice to each other."

"Please sign me out of here."

Jessica retreated. "Sonny, I can't take any more of this!" she said. "Okay, maybe I don't know how you feel. But can you imagine how I feel? If I tried to kill myself, would you let me do it?"

"If I knew you were dying?"

"Yes."

"Of course," Sonny said without hesitation.

"You really would?"

"If I knew you were going to suffer."

"Sonny?" Jessica said, pleading with him with her eyes.

Sonny looked at her, looked at her hard. She was a good women, a friend. They had been pals and lovers; she was the mother of his child. Could he really? Would he really? And with a sigh of resignation he returned to the bed, got in, and covered himself with the sheet.

"No," he said, his voice very low. "I couldn't."

And Jessica was on him then, half lying across him, her arms around his neck, and without thinking, Sonny was holding her tightly to his chest, stroking her back, stroking her cheek, wiping away her tears, kissing her hair.

"Oh, Sonny," she sobbed, "let's stop hurting each other. Please. Let's stop . . . right now . . . forever."

And Sonny sat up then and pulled her even tighter to him, and they were hugging and rocking, and Jessica's tears must have been contagious because Sonny could feel moisture on his own cheeks, and he knew he was crying, crying for Jessica, and for himself, and for the crazy turn of fate that had brought them to this scene, and because even as he heard himself mutter a promise to Jessica, he knew he wouldn't keep it, because the pain was coming again, and he wasn't going to—couldn't —continue to live with it.

Chapter Seven

SONNY FELT HIS CHIN AND CHEEKS. He hadn't shaved for many days. It wasn't exactly a beard yet, but it wasn't stubble any longer, either. Jessica had tried to talk him into growing a beard on several occasions. She was finally going to get her way. The bitch! There had to be a way to reach her! Maybe the next time. She had been here three times—no, four times—and she would come again, and one of these times she'd weaken. He wondered if she had told Julie yet. He wondered if Dr. Kling would keep his promise, and if he would be allowed to go outside today. The IV had been out at least a day. He wondered if it was morning or afternoon. The blinds were down.

Gingerly he checked his left arm. The inside of the crook was still very tender. How long had they kept him tied to the bed with the IV dripping after the fight he had put up about it? That he still hadn't been able to figure out.

Sonny shook his head. When he woke to find the IV out, he couldn't tell if it was morning or afternoon, either, and at some point, when he was still too groggy to even open his eyes, a nurse had unceremoniously ordered him onto his stomach and jabbed a needle into his butt. He hadn't really cared. He had been in too much pain and feeling too weak to resist. His sleep

since he'd been here had been restless, dream-filled, un-
pleasant, except for a half-remembered sequence in-
volving an unctuous man in a suit carrying a briefcase,
with a sign around his neck which read INSURANCE
MAN. The man had come running up to Sonny at the
edge of a baseball diamond where he had been watching Julie, unsupervised, dancing in her leotard around
the pitcher's mound. The man had pressed a card into
Sonny's hand and offered him money on which to live
if he would make a settlement on his insurance policies.
Booker had been there, wearing a dwarf uniform, and
Sonny had ordered him to remove the man, who
promptly tried to sell Booker a policy which he called
"Midget Protection." No, it hadn't been quite a dream.
He remembered calling Booker a midget when the beds
were being shifted in the rooms. All of the mechanical
beds had been removed. It had been Booker who had
helped him move to the new bed.

Sonny got up then and opened the blinds. Yes, it was
definitely morning. He took a deep breath, then another,
and tentatively tried a deep knee bend. He was rusty,
still weak, but it wasn't so bad. And he was hungry!
Hungry!

The room seemed much larger now, with its single
bed, and again, sometime while he was asleep, someone
had left a plastic glass filled with water on the night
table. Sonny pulled the only chair in the room over to
the window and sat down, resting his feet on the windowsill and slowly sipping the water.

There were six—no, seven—people visible through
the window, including a white-coated attendant. The
others—four men and two women—were all dressed
in pajamas and gowns and robes. One of them, a woman with half-grown-out bleached hair, was obviously
nuts; she was standing under a tree wringing her hands,
and Sonny chuckled without amusement as she slowly
began to remove her robe and then unbutton the top of

her pajamas. The woman sitting on the bench, a young-ish woman, turned her head away; so did both the men standing near the fence and the man who was walking. The elderly man sitting on a bench beyond the trees, near a clump of bushes, didn't even shift position, but continued to stare in front of him. The attendant was gentle with the woman as he led her away.

Two new people sauntered across the scene in front of him, a middle-aged man and Booker, who was guid-ing the man about, obviously acquainting him with the grounds. Sonny wondered if he, too, would get a guided tour.

And then the door opened, and Dr. Kling was there, followed by an orderly who was carrying a tray.

The smell of toast and coffee got Sonny to his feet. Breakfast was his favorite meal. He was almost always hungry in the morning. It used to drive Jessica crazy. She could barely tolerate the smell of coffee before eleven.

"Good!" Dr. Kling said. "Your appetite has returned. Would you like to stay by the window? You can hold the tray on your lap."

"Okay," Sonny said. He returned to the chair.

"Do you feel well enough to take a short walk around the grounds today?"

"Yes," Sonny said. And right out of here if I can.

"Good!" Dr. Kling said. "Eat now, and then some-one will come and take you outside to get some exer-cise."

"Fine," Sonny said, taking the tray. Toast! Coffee! Cereal! Stewed fruit! A small container of cream! Slow-ly he poured the coffee into the cup; it was weak but aromatic. Slowly he raised a spoonful of cereal to his mouth. It tasted good. Very good.

He finished the breakfast down to the last crumb, eating slowly, enjoying it, watching the activity on the grounds. The old man who sat on the bench near the bushes still hadn't moved, hadn't even turned his head.

Sonny took the last sip of coffee, put the tray on the bed, and used the bathroom to wash and freshen up. He felt his chin again. Three or four more days and the beard would be quite respectable. He wondered what it looked like, although he could summon up a picture of himself in college the only time he had kept a beard for any length of time. His whole sophomore year. The year he had dated Shirley Schuber, the German girl who had loved to give him hand jobs in the car.

"Are you done with your food, Mr. Lawson?"

Booker was in the room. Yes, he did remind Sonny of a dwarf. It wasn't that he was misshapen, it was that the muscularity of his body seemed as if it should belong on a much taller man. He wasn't even that short —five-six, at least—but his chest was decidedly barrel-shaped, and he wore the sleeves of his attendant's uniform rolled up to expose his biceps, which were developed in a way that Sonny associated with the lifting of weights.

"Yes," Sonny said.

"Good. Now if you'll please put on your robe, Dr. Kling has asked me to show you the grounds."

"What robe?" Sonny asked.

Booker gave him a look that made Sonny furious, and opened the closet door. There was indeed a robe there, and a spare set of slippers, and Sonny opened the drawers in the dresser and discovered a spare pair of pajamas and three small, clean towels. Not long enough to hang himself with, he noticed, which was actually just as well. He hated the idea of hanging. He wondered when the clothes had been put into the room. Probably when the water glass had been refilled.

He pulled on the robe and let Booker guide him down the hall and out the door beyond the reception area and attendant's cubicle.

Another beautiful Santa Barbara day.

It felt good to be outside. It was warm, and the sun was quite bright. Sonny blinked his eyes against the glare, and slowed down a bit. He really wasn't quite as strong as he had thought. Booker let him stand for a minute, and named the buildings for him, and pointed out the bridge that led to the park area beyond, which was off limits to Sonny until he was approved by Dr. Kling, and then Booker had his arm and was dragging him off in the direction of a bench near the bridge.

"Quit dragging me around, Booker! This is supposed to be exercise for me, not your arm."

Booker relaxed his hold on Sonny's arm a bit, and Sonny dragged his feet. The bench he was being led to was across the yard from a clump of bushes. Sonny stopped walking and pulled his arm away from Booker. He raised his arms above his head and stretched; God, but his back muscles were tight!

"Is that the reason you went into nursing?" Sonny said. "Because you like to drag people around?"

Booker was obviously used to being berated verbally by the patients he tended at La Playa, because he didn't bother to respond. He just took hold of Sonny's arm again, dragged him to the bench, and pushed him down on the wooden seat.

"Now," Booker said, "I am going to take a fifteen-minute break and go have a cigarette. You are free to walk as far as the bridge in that direction, and up to the edge of the flower bed near the Administration Building. Don't worry, someone will be keeping an eye on you. Dr. Kling said you could have half an hour, but if you're good I'll let you have a few minutes more."

"You know why you're so aggressive, Booker? It's because you're so short. You're sort of an ugly Tom Thumb."

Booker seemed on the verge of saying something, but he obviously wanted his break more than he wanted to make a scene, and he left Sonny without another word, waving at Carl and walking across the lawn.

Sonny waited until the two men disappeared around the side of the first cottage, and then sauntered across the lawn to the bench where the old man sat, near the clump of trees. His eyes roamed the grounds; there was nothing and nobody that looked familiar.

The old man did not acknowledge Sonny's presence when he sat on the edge of the bench, and they sat silently for a few minutes. The traffic on the street outside the barbed-wire fence was not heavy, but it was traffic nevertheless, and it reminded Sonny that the people in the cars were out there, free, and he was in here, and not free. It made him angry.

"This place is nothing but a fancy prison!" he said to the old man.

"Absolutely," the old man said, without moving or changing his expression.

"I'd sure as hell like to get out of here. Wouldn't you?"

"Oh, absolutely," the old man said. Sonny looked in the direction in which the old man was staring, but he couldn't figure out what the man was looking at. Was he trying to spot someone in one of the windows of the middle building?

Sonny ran a scan on the building but didn't spot anything out of the ordinary. It all seemed strange. He wondered which building was Marlon's. Booker hadn't pointed out anything called the South Wing. It must be a section in one of the buildings. He wondered if the old man was staring at the windows because of the bars. Perhaps he had thought of a way. . . .

"I have a toxic blood disease," Sonny confided, trying to draw the man out. "No chance of survival. Zip . . . you know what I mean?"

"Absolutely," the old man said.

"Wouldn't you want to kill yourself under those circumstances?"

"Absolutely!" the old man said.

Sonny felt a surge of elation. He had been right! He relaxed into the hardwood back of the bench and crossed his arms and his legs, brooding.

"Absolutely!" the old man said.

Sonny looked at him. He was still staring at the side of the building.

"Absolutely," the old man said again.

"Oh, shit. You're as crazy as everybody else around here."

"Absolutely," he chimed in as the old man opened his mouth to speak the word again.

It was at this point that Sonny caught the slight movement in the bushes behind him, and even as he turned his head to get a better view, Marlon's face appeared.

"Marlon!" Sonny said.

"Quiet. Don't look over this way. Just get up and pretend you're looking at the bushes," Marlon said. "I'll keep an eye out for Booker."

"What about the old man?" Sonny said.

"He's no problem," Marlon said.

"Absolutely," the old man said.

Sonny got up slowly, bending down once to touch his toes, and then moved around behind the bench to stand at the edge of the clump of bushes. Marlon was crouching in a small clearing in the center. He must have entered the bushes from the far side, from a spot concealed from view by trees.

"How'd you escape?" Sonny asked.

"I forget," Marlon said. "I forget a lot of things just as soon as I do them."

"You're lucky," Sonny said.

He was fingering the leaves on a bush, and shifted position slightly when a middle-aged woman in a bright red robe suddenly got up from a bench and began walking in his direction. She stopped when Sonny moved, hesitated, then returned to her bench. Sonny remained at an angle to the bushes so that he could keep an eye on her.

"How are you doing, Sonny?" Marlon asked.

"Not so good," Sonny confessed.

"Yeah," Marlon said, "I heard about the bed. You should never use my dumb ideas. Out of the mouths of Polacks—"

"Stop that, Marlon!" Sonny said, his voice sharper than he had intended. Marlon pushed deeper into the bushes, as if hurt by the tone of Sonny's voice. "It would've worked if they hadn't caught me," Sonny said. "It was a good idea. It hurt a lot, though, and it didn't work. I wish I could think of some way to do it that didn't hurt."

"I've got another idea," Marlon said. "Why don't you walk around the back of those trees and come and join me here? I'll keep a lookout this way."

"You're on!" Sonny said. The old man on the bench hadn't moved. There wasn't an attendant in sight. The woman who had started to walk in his direction earlier was heading toward the park area on the other side of the footbridge. Sonny rounded the side of the trees and quickly squatted down, out of sight. Marlon inched his way through the little clearing and held the branches aside for Sonny, and then the two men were squatting on their haunches in the safety of the clearing in the middle of the bushes.

"Okay, Marlon," Sonny said, keeping his voice low. "What's on your mind?"

"Uhh . . ."

"Come on," Sonny said. "Give!"

"Okay, okay," Marlon said. "I've always thought that jumping out of a window would be kind of painless . . . except for the last part." He looked at Sonny

133

with his wide, round eyes, obviously asking for approval of his statement.

"Yeah," Sonny said. "At least it would be quick. I couldn't change my mind." He thought about it for a few seconds; Marlon's eyes never left his face, although his expression changed several times. "I'd do it right now," Sonny said finally. "But how can I do it? The buildings are all low, and besides, all the windows have bars."

"There's the tower," Marlon said, pointing in the direction of the Administration Building.

"Sure, Marlon," Sonny said. "Except that it's in the Administration Building, and it doesn't have any windows."

"Yes, it does," Marlon said triumphantly.

Sonny looked at him, hope dawning.

"There's a single window on the other side. You just can't see it from here. I've never been up there, but an attendant a year or so ago told me that it could be reached through a door on the fifth floor, which is empty. I've been saving the idea for the right moment. We could sneak in the basement entrance and avoid the first floor altogether, because there's an inside fire escape that bypasses the first floor. The only danger would be if we were spotted entering the building, or on the third floor, because I understand that one of the orderlies is using a room on the third floor to meet with Miss Martin, the afternoon nurse. Have you met her?"

"I don't think so," Sonny said, his eyes on the tower. It was at least five stories high, and there was a large bell on a scaffold at the top. He hadn't heard the bell ring a single time, but there would have to be an entrance into the tower. And Marlon wouldn't lie about the window. Just because he couldn't see it from here didn't mean that it didn't exist.

"You'd remember if you'd met her," Marlon said, shaking his head and rolling his eyes. "Ooh-la-la!"

"Shove it, Marlon," Sonny said. "This is no time to be thinking about dames. Now how do we go about getting there?"

"Follow me," Marlon said, spreading the branches and cautiously inching his way out of the thicket.

When they reached the side of the trees and realized that no attendants were in sight, Marlon and Sonny simply walked across the lawn to the back of Sonny's building, keeping twenty yards apart.

It was so simple, such a piece of cake getting into the Administration Building that Sonny could hardly believe it. Once, on the landing to the third floor, Marlon pulled back and put his fingers to his lips, and they both froze as the sound of footsteps coming down a corridor reached their ears. But the footsteps didn't even hesitate at the door to the stairs, and on the landing of the fourth floor Marlon took his fingers from his lips.

"We've got it made!" he said. "No one comes up here. No one at all. The fourth floor is a storage area, and the fifth floor is actually boarded shut except for this corridor."

They were in the corridor then, a narrow, dark space with the only light coming from a large crack underneath a door at the far end. Sonny held the door of the fire stairs open while Marlon walked ahead to test the door.

Marlon was back at his side almost immediately.

"The door's locked," he said.

Sonny nearly groaned.

"But I think I can get it open," Marlon said. Then he was down at the far end of the corridor again, and there was an audible click, and light flooded the corridor. Sonny quickly released the fire escape door and joined Marlon.

They were in a small circular room in the tower. And yes, there was a window. It was not barred. In the ceiling over their heads was a trapdoor which Sonny realized must lead to the bell.

"Look," Sonny said after checking out the window, "maybe I should climb up into the bell tower and jump from there. There's no ledge on the window. I wish there was a ledge to jump off. In the movies, there's always a ledge."

"That would just give you another place to stand and talk yourself out of it. Go on, Sonny . . . all you have to do is jump."

"Boy, you sure are anxious," Sonny said, walking back to the window and looking out again. The side wall of the tower was solid and straight, and below was nothing but hard ground.

"I'm sorry," Marlon said. "It just seems like it's what you really want. You keep saying you want somebody to believe you."

"You're right, Marlon," Sonny said. "I'm going to jump." He looked down again, remembering his failures. "It might not be high enough to kill me, though," he said.

"There's only one way to find out," Marlon said.

Sonny nodded and looked out again. It wasn't any different from taking the pills, really, he thought. All he had to do was do it. All he had to do was put one leg out of the window, then straddle the sill and pull the other leg on out. And that would have him jumping feet first, and it would cut the distance to the ground. He looked again. No, it really might not be high enough to kill him.

"Well, you're not even going to hurt yourself if you *crawl* down," Marlon said, urging him on.

Sonny was sitting on the windowsill now, his legs dangling out, but he couldn't seem to summon the energy to make the final move.

"Come on, Sonny!" Marlon's voice was high-pitched now with nervous excitement. "Give up! You can do it!"

"What if I just land on my feet and break my ankles? Then I'd have a blood disease and broken ankles. What good would that do?"

"You want me to drop you on your head?" Marlon asked, coming to stand by Sonny's side. "C'mon," he said, "I'll drop you on your head. Come back in, and lean out, and I'll grab hold of your ankles and drop you on your head. C'mon!"

"Wait a minute, Marlon, I've got to think about this." Sonny retreated from the window. "If you drop me on my head and I make it, you could be charged with murder."

"I've already been convicted of murder," Marlon said.

"Yeah," Sonny said. "That makes sense. But are you sure you want to get involved? Why should you want to get involved? They'll make things very tough for you."

"Did you mean it when you said you liked me?" Marlon asked then.

"Yes," Sonny said. "I did."

"Okay," Marlon said, throwing his hands apart in a gesture of supplication. "I've wanted to help a lot of people, but no one has let me. Please. I want to help."

Sonny gave Marlon a hard look. His eyes were gleaming, and there was perspiration on his upper lip, which was trembling as if controlled by a mechanism different from the mechanism which controlled his hands. His hands were at his sides, opening and closing, clenching at the fabric of his long nightshirt, which was covered with a gray robe. He was obviously in a state of excitation, and he was just as equally serious about his offer.

"Okay," Sonny said finally. "But how are we going to do it?"

"Here," Marlon said. "Kneel down and put your head out and lean your chest out as far as you can. I'll

pick up your ankles, and you can help balance yourself with your hands. When I've got your feet out, I'll
just let go."

"Okay," Sonny said, kneeling down and sticking his
head out of the window. "Easy."

"Point your head straight down," Marlon said.

"I can't," Sonny said. "You're pushing too hard."
With his hands he was pushing against the side of the
tower, but he couldn't seem to keep his head down.
The ground was spinning beneath him.

"Wait!" Sonny yelled then. "It's not high enough!"

"Sure it is," Marlon said. "Are you ready? Shall I
let go?"

"No," Sonny yelled in terror. "No. Don't do it! Lift
me back up. Right now, Marlon. Lift me back up!"

Sonny heard Marlon sigh, and then he was being
pulled back inside the window.

"What'd you pull me in for?" Sonny yelled when
he was back inside, his feet safely on the floor.

"You asked me to," Marlon said, puffing, a bit out
of breath, suddenly confused.

"Marlon, don't listen to me! I need you because I
haven't got the guts to do this thing myself. You
shouldn't have pulled me back in, you should have
just let go! What good are you! This is never going to
work if you listen to me!"

"I'm sorry," Marlon said. "I'm sorry. Really I am.
I failed you."

Sonny looked away in exasperation as Marlon said,
"Typical!" in a different voice, then, "Shut up!" then
hit himself on the cheek. Sonny was standing back a
few paces from the window; the distance to the ground
seemed further away. Perhaps . . .

"You know, Marlon, we can still do it," Sonny said
slowly.

"How?" Marlon said, obviously eager to rectify his
mistake.

"Push me out," Sonny said. "I'll stand in front of

the window and you just push me out. That way I won't have to think. I won't look at you or anything, and I'll try not to brace myself."

"That's a good idea," Marlon said. "I'll do it with pleasure." Indeed, little dancing lights seemed to appear in Marlon's eyes. Sonny turned away from him, uneasy, and went to stand squarely in front of the window, closing his eyes and trying to make his muscles go limp. But at the first touch of Marlon's hands his body automatically resisted, his arms reaching out with a volition of their own to grab hold of the window frame.

"Maybe it's not high enough," he said.

"Quit resisting!" Marlon said.

"I'll try, Marlon."

And then Sonny heard Marlon retreat into the small room and then begin a charge in his direction, not running exactly, but coming fast, and at the last possible instant he stepped aside and watched with horror as Marlon, as if in a slow-motion sequence, tried to stop his momentum but was unable to, and then his head, then his torso, and then his legs disappeared out the window. Sonny made a desperate lunge for Marlon's legs, grabbing the end of his nightshirt instead, which held for a second before the fabric slipped through his fingers.

Marlon's scream seemed to hang in the air of the beautiful Santa Barbara day.

Shaking quite uncontrollably, Sonny forced himself to stick his head out the window and look down.

Booker and Carl were standing beneath the window, checking themselves for injuries, and Marlon was lying on the ground, sprawled in a crumpled heap, his right wrist at a peculiar angle. He was moaning, but he was obviously alive, and even as Sonny watched, Booker gave Marlon a little nudge with the toe of his shoe, then looked up and began quickly walking around towards the front of the Administration Building, obviously coming for Sonny. Marlon rolled over on his back.

"You're right," he said to Sonny. "It's not high enough."

Chapter Eight

SONNY HAD NOT TOUCHED HIS FOOD. For the first time since he had been admitted to La Playa, his door was locked. It was an outrage that made him seethe. He stared out the window, resisting an impulse to shake the bars, to open the window further and grasp the bars with two hands and pull them free. . . . He watched helplessly as Marlon was walked across the yard to his building, a bandage on his head, his wrist in a cast, not limping, but obviously in pain.

He supposed that he was in for some disciplinary action, but he could not imagine what they had in store for him. *They* were no longer faceless. *They* were Jessica and Marty, and Dr. Kling, and Carl and all the other attendants, and particularly Booker, who came through the door now, refastening a hook full of keys onto the loop on his belt, alone, in control of the situation even though he was alone and half a head shorter than Sonny.

"You didn't eat, Mr. Lawson," Booker said, helping himself to a cookie. "That's not going to help. You can't starve yourself in here. If you try, we'll just tie you back on the bed and stick another IV in your arm. Now come along, Dr. Maneet wants to see you. You're becoming famous, did you know that? Two unique suicide tries in less than a week. Keep it up and you'll be in real trouble."

"You're not just short, Booker," Sonny said.

"You're also squat. Some men can carry off being short. But nobody likes a squat person."

But Booker just smiled, having heard all of the possible insults already, Sonny realized, and before Booker could cross the room and lay hands on him, he shrugged and went to the closet to get his robe. The spare slippers had disappeared. Had he overlooked a possibility? He looked at his slippers. Was there a way to use them?

Turning over the idea in his head, Sonny allowed Booker to walk him down the hall, out the door, and across the yard to the Administration Building. Who was Dr. Maneet? Was there something the matter with Dr. Kling, or would he be seeing a different person each time he was summoned? He didn't know, and, he realized, he didn't really care. All he cared about was *getting out*. It was true that the medication they had been giving him since he had been admitted to La Playa had gotten the pain in his stomach more or less under control. He had not had a pain greater than a two—or a two and a half—since the one that had made him collapse in Dr. Kling's office. But there was an almost constant dull ache in his stomach and side now, and he knew it wasn't going to get any better.

Three doors down the hall from the main admissions office was a door with a sign that read: DR. WILSON MANEET, DEATH THERAPY.

"Here's a guy who's carved out a fun career for himself," Sonny said as Booker stopped and knocked on the door.

"Come in."

Booker opened the door and ushered Sonny inside.

Seated behind a desk was a man in his mid-fifties, a robust, cheerful-looking man with a full head of gray-brown hair. The room was dominated by the autographed pictures, framed letters, and certificates of awards that covered most of the wall surfaces above the waistline. In one corner were two file cabinets, the top drawer of one of them open. In the other corner was an exercise machine and a ten-pound barbell. From behind the curtains on the window peeked a tennis racket. The wall across from the desk was lined with floor-to-ceiling bookcases, crammed with books and piles of papers and pamphlets.

"Hello," Dr. Maneet said.

"This is Mr. Lawson. I'll be outside," Booker said.

"You'll always be outside, Booker," Sonny said. "And you'll be too short to look in." Sonny was surprised to see that his remark had caused Dr. Maneet to suppress a laugh. It depressed him. He had an awful feeling that he was going to like this man, and to like this man would be dangerous.

"Have a seat, Mr. Lawson," the doctor said. "I'm Dr. Maneet." He stood for a moment and offered Sonny his hand.

Sonny returned the shake unenthusiastically.

"And you're going to try to talk me into living," Sonny said sourly.

"No, I'm not," Dr. Maneet said, toying with the papers in the folder on his desk. "As I understand it, you're definitely going to die."

Dr. Maneet's statement shocked Sonny, sending his body's temperature mechanism through changes, first cold and then flashing hot. "Well . . ." He stopped. "That's a weird thing to say," he managed finally.

"Is it? Why?" Dr. Maneet asked.

"Well . . . I mean, it's the truth," Sonny said, "but nobody's come out and said it. I mean, nobody except me."

Dr. Maneet was watching him with kindly eyes, and Sonny looked away from the man to the framed letters and photos on the wall. He recognized none of the faces and none of the names. Ordinary people all, but the dedications were full of love and hope. Here was a man who was obviously respected, not only by people in his profession but by his patients as well.

Dr. Maneet waited quietly until Sonny returned his attention to him. "People tend to coddle or cover up things when someone they love is ill," he said. "It makes it easier for them."

"Screw them," Sonny said automatically.

"I agree with you," Dr. Maneet said. "One of the worst aspects of dying is that it's so lonely. People are unable or afraid to share your grief."

"Lonely . . . that's right," Sonny agreed. "You can't imagine how lonely."

"I don't have to imagine it. I'm dying, too."

Dr. Maneet articulated his sentence casually, but the impact hit Sonny like a body blow.

"*You're* dying?"

"Yep," Dr. Maneet said, a conspiratorial grin on his face. "The doctors tell me I could go any time . . . just like that." He snapped his fingers for emphasis. "Of course, they told me that over two years ago."

Dr. Maneet got up and stretched, locking his hands behind his back and bringing them up as far as he could, bending slightly at the waist, then rolling his shoulders about as if to relieve sore muscles. Sonny watched him, momentarily speechless, trying to absorb what was happening. This man was also dying, and Sonny realized that his own attitude of hostility had vanished, that he was now feeling confused. Dr. Maneet looked healthy; he sounded healthy; his mental attitude was healthy; Sonny began to doubt himself.

"But you seem . . . so alive," he said helplessly.

"Yes," Dr. Maneet agreed, "it's strange. I'm not always this robust, but right now I seem to be in a period of total remission. I even played tennis yesterday."

"Did you win?"

"No," the doctor said, shaking his head. "I played shitty. But I also played shitty when I was well."

"What have you got?"

"Heart trouble," Dr. Maneet said. "Lots of heart trouble."

"I don't see how you can keep working," Sonny said.

"I couldn't at first. I dropped my private practice. But then I just kept on living . . . and it got pretty boring."

"Were you a death therapist before?" Sonny asked.

"No," Dr. Maneet said. "I've gotten into this line of work as the result of my own problems. I think you should start coming to the death therapy sessions."

"No, I don't think so," Sonny said. "I'm not going to be here long enough for it to matter."

"It might help. The fact is, I don't know if it's helping anybody else, but it sure is helping me. I think my work is what's keeping me alive."

"You're lucky," Sonny said. "I sell real estate. Real estate never kept anybody alive. In fact, it killed a few friends of mine." Why was he talking to this man? If he wasn't careful, he was going to end up liking him. He was too young to be a father figure, but his friendliness and sincerity had reached Sonny, and he doubted if it was simply the fact that Dr. Maneet was also living on the limbo edge of the constant awareness of death. There was about him a vitality and a humanity that would be rare under any circumstance.

"You know," Sonny said, "you're the first doctor I haven't hated since I got sick."

Dr. Maneet laughed. The sound was contagious, and Sonny felt himself smiling.

The doctor was looking at the file on his desk now. "You were active in sports, weren't you?" the doctor said.

"In high school and college. I played baseball and was a pretty good diver."

"Do you still do either one of them?"

"No, of course not," Sonny said. "Oh, I'll take a dive off a board at a pool sometimes to show off, and

I like the ocean. I like to bodysurf a lot. But I don't play baseball at all. I was a pitcher, but nowhere near good enough to make a go of it professionally. There's no place for an adult to play baseball just for fun."

"Sure, there is," Dr. Maneet said. "Neighborhood teams, that sort of thing."

"Not in my neighborhood," Sonny said. "I haven't got a neighborhood."

"Do you feel sorry for yourself often?"

"You just sounded like Dr. Kling," Sonny said. "He asked me that, too."

"Well, it's an obvious question under the circumstances, don't you think?"

"No, I don't think," Sonny said. Dr. Maneet was holding the top paper in the file. There was a smaller piece of paper clipped to the top. "Is that a report from Dr. Kling?" Sonny asked.

"Yes, it is."

"What does it say?"

"It's a summary of your medical history, and an opinion."

"An opinion about what?"

Dr. Maneet tilted back in his chair and cocked his head to one side. "About how you should be treated."

"I know how I should be treated!" Sonny said. "I should be let out of here. Now."

"No, not now," Dr. Maneet said. "Now we are talking so that I can add to the file and give *my* opinion." He looked at Sonny thoughtfully, brought his chair back to the vertical, tore a piece of paper from a small pad, and stuck it under the slip on Dr. Kling's report. He looked at Sonny one more time, then reached for the desk pen that was held in an onyx base. It was a fountain pen, Sonny noticed. He hadn't seen one of those for a while.

Dr. Maneet began to write, shielding the paper from Sonny's eyes with his left hand.

Sonny began to fidget.

"What are you writing?"

"My opinion."

"But we've hardly talked!" Sonny protested. "How can you write an opinion when we've hardly talked?"

"We've talked."

"No, we haven't! I haven't told you how I feel about all of this."

"Yes, you have," Dr. Maneet said, "except you have also told me that you've made up your mind not to listen."

"Let me see that," Sonny said, grabbing the paper from Dr. Maneet. He glanced at the note. The doctor's handwriting was beautiful. "You play dirty," Sonny said.

Dr. Maneet shrugged. "The stakes are high . . . life and death."

Sonny looked at the note again: *Patient needs— 1. A home. 2. Love. 3. A day of bodysurfing. 4. A pitcher's mitt for his next birthday.* Slowly he tore the note into pieces the size of a torn parking ticket and got up to drop them in the wastepaper basket, not returning to the chair, but pacing around the room. He was feeling caged, totally out of control of the situation. He took his frustration out on the wastebasket, kicking it over, and then, unable to face Dr. Maneet, he went to stand near the door, looking at the bookcase wall. He was caught! There was nothing he could do. He had stood like this in high school once, after having been caught cheating on a math test. But he was an adult now, not a boy of fifteen, and his life was over, not beginning. Then the stakes had seemed much higher.

"I'm sorry," he said at last, turning around to face the doctor. "I just . . . I just want to be put out of my misery, that's all. Jesus, they do that for a horse."

Sonny knew that the look of understanding on the doctor's face was heartfelt, but so was the man's undeniable conviction that living was the answer. Well,

147

they'd had a disagreement, that was all. Nothing that couldn't be worked out.

"See, Dr. Maneet, I'm terrified of pain. Haircuts hurt me," Sonny said, to see if an attempt at humor would help.

"Sonny, what makes you so convinced your death is going to be painful? Have you ever actually seen someone die?"

"I had an aunt that died, but I never really saw her much after she went in the hospital."

Dr. Maneet nodded. "That's one of the reasons people in our culture are so frightened of dying. We never see what it's actually like. We hide death behind walls."

"I remember being kind of glad when they took my aunt away," Sonny confessed. "I was tired of finding wadded up Kleenexes everywhere."

"Death can be a strain on the family, but it also strengthens it. People should die at home," Dr. Maneet said with absolute conviction.

He must have a nice home, Sonny thought. A wife who loves him, a couple of kids, maybe, neighbors who probably drop in all the time just to make sure that he's still alive. It made Sonny jealous. "If I wanted to die at home, I'd have to hustle between my ex-wife and kid's house, my girl friend's house, and my place. I'd probably die in a taxi."

"Are your parents alive, Sonny?"

"No," Sonny said, and then realized what he'd meant. They'd been dead for him for years, hadn't they? The clarification of that fact made him very unhappy. "I meant to say yes," Sonny said. "I guess it's because they've never really treated me like I thought a son should be treated, and I guess I made what is called a Freudian slip."

"Either that or a boo-boo," Dr. Maneet said with a twinkle in his eyes, and Sonny laughed, a real laugh, a good, booming laugh. Dr. Maneet was laughing, too, as if he were never again going to be excluded from

148

anything that looked like fun, and even as he laughed Sonny realized that it was the first time he had done so since the morning he had seen Dr. Krugman. The thought was instantly sobering, but he felt better; some unidentified tension had eased. He touched his chin. God, would he like a mirror! The beard felt as if it was nearly right. Soon—if he lived that long—if he could figure out how—he would have to groom it.

"Why don't you at least come to one death therapy session?" Dr. Maneet asked then. "Just sitting around talking to people like yourself can make death less crazy. Maybe even meaningful."

Sonny shook his head; Dr. Maneet responded with a have-it-your-own-way shrug and got up from behind the desk.

"Okay," the doctor said. "I'll let you out of here, but I want you to at least read a pamphlet. Okay?"

"Sure," Sonny said. That was easy enough.

Dr. Maneet crossed to the wall of bookcases behind Sonny and began thumbing through the piles of literature that occupied the shelves. They were in untidy stacks. He was whistling, an act so simple and yet so startling that Sonny found himself staring at the man's back. He could not conceive of attaining the peace of mind that would ever allow him to whistle again. Dr. Maneet was staring at the piles of papers on the shelves, and he had scratched his chin. Then, unexpectedly, he looked up and, just as unexpectedly, took a little leap into the air, attempting to reach a pile of pamphlets on the top shelf. The motion brought heightened color to his face. Before Sonny could help, Dr. Maneet had jumped again, bringing down a pile of pamphlets, which he bent to retrieve. He made the first disagreeable sound Sonny had heard since he had entered the office, and prepared to jump again.

"Hey, never mind," Sonny said, amazed at the man's persistence. "Maybe I'll just come to one of your sessions." It couldn't hurt, could it?

"Really?" The doctor's face had gotten slightly paler, but the signs of exertion were still clearly visible.

"What the hell," Sonny said. "I can't imagine spending another happy minute, but you're dying, too, and you're the happiest sonofabitch I've ever seen. You were actually whistling. Dying, and *actually whistling.*" Yes, this really was a man to admire, and if he could do it. . . . "I'll give it a shot," Sonny said, and was rewarded with a smile of unfeigned happiness on the doctor's face.

"It's a good decision, Sonny," the doctor said.

Sonny shrugged. "You're a hell of a salesman." Yes, he was. He would have sold thousands of sites for Lake Crest Estates. But it was a tenuous agreement, Sonny knew, depending on this man and his good humor. One bad remark, one moment of wavering or weakness on his part . . . "I'm going to need your help to hang in," Sonny said, meaning every word of it.

"I'm not going anywhere," Dr. Maneet said, and winked.

Sonny felt his face break into a smile, and impulsively he stuck out his hand for a shake. He liked this man. This man could be a friend. The hand that returned his clasp was strong and reliable, and even as Sonny was thinking this, Dr. Maneet let out a small gasp, and his hand clutched and then loosened in Sonny's. Sonny threw out his arms to support the man as his eyes rolled to the top of his head and he began slowly to sink to the ground.

He was dead.

There was no doubt at all in Sonny's mind. He just *knew.*

He was back to the beginning, all over again.

"Come in here, Booker," Sonny yelled at the top of his voice.

Dr. Maneet's hand was still in his, and slowly Sonny released his pressure. The arm fell.

Sonny walked to the door and yanked it open. Booker was leaning against the far wall, staring into space.

"Booker, I hate to interrupt your dreams of being tall," Sonny snarled, "but you better get in here. Dr. Maneet—"

Booker was across the hall and into the office before Sonny finished his sentence, and quickly he knelt at the doctor's side.

"What did you do to him?" Booker asked, showing the first human emotions Sonny had seen the man exhibit.

What did I do to him? Sonny thought. I made him think he had a convert, and. . . . "I liked him," Sonny said.

And the day just got worse.

He was taken to use the library facilities and was unable to cut his wrist with paper.

The medication they gave him made him groggy, and he was unable to convince Jessica to let him out when she came to visit, and, worst of all, she had brought a gift from Julie.

Depressed.

He was so depressed.

But at least an attendant had come and allowed him this second period of time outside. It was better being up and moving around than confined to his room.

Julie had sent him a whole box of Twinkies and a note that nearly broke his heart:

Dear Daddy:

Mommy has told me that you are in the hospital but that you are all right. I am glad you are all right, but I wish that you hadn't lied to me. Mommy says you might have a telephone soon. I hope so, because I miss you. I don't think it's fair

that I can't come to visit. Please get well soon and
come home *soon*. I'll go play miniature golf with
you if you want.

Love, Julie

Sonny walked across the lawn to the clump of
bushes near the benches on the off chance that Marlon
had escaped again. He wasn't there. The old man that
Sonny had dubbed the Absolutely King was sitting on
his usual bench, as well as a young woman Sonny had
never seen before. She was in her early twenties and
had a pretty face and was pawing at the ground with
the toe of her right slipper, totally engrossed in her
task.

He walked toward the back of the grounds and stood
for a minute or two on the bridge that crossed the
pond, watching the swans gliding, moving beyond to sit
beneath a weeping willow tree when the groundskeeper,
a middle-aged Japanese man, steered his truck onto the
bridge heading for the park area beyond. Sonny
watched him for a while as he stopped, leaving the
trunk door open, and began to unload manure sacks
and some medium-sized shrubs in an area near the
fence.

It was such a tranquil scene. He unwrapped the two
Twinkies he had put in his bathrobe pocket and broke
them into pieces, throwing the pieces slowly to the
swans who glided effortlessly on the clear water of the
pond. It was a scene Dr. Maneet would have appre-
ciated, Sonny thought ruefully, puckering up his mouth
and attempting to whistle. But the sound that came out
sounded harsh to his ears. How could he whistle a tune
when he couldn't think of a single song he wanted to
hear?

And then, not knowing how he knew it, Sonny
sensed that Marlon was behind the tree. How did he do

it? Sonny wondered, not turning around but holding half a Twinkie out behind his back.

Marlon came from behind the tree and stood beside Sonny, silently taking the Twinkie. Sonny threw another piece to the swams and looked at his friend. Marlon's wrist was in a cast. There was a bruise on his forehead and a scrape on his left cheek, but he was smiling with pleasure, and Sonny motioned for him to sit beside him on the bank of the pond.

"Dying didn't seem to hurt Dr. Maneet at all," Sonny said. "He just looked funny and then keeled over." He shook his head. "But up until then he was happy. He found reasons to live. Maybe watching two swans is reason enough to stay alive."

Marlon shrugged and happily nibbled at his Twinkie. Sonny looked fondly at the swans, and threw the last piece of the sweet to them. Without warning they were fighting over it, pecking away at each other, their wings spreading to full width, getting vicious and making noises and heading for the bank. Sonny quickly got up and helped Marlon to his feet, and the men went to stand by the trunk of the willow tree.

"Oh, God, isn't that depressing!" Sonny said. The swans had come out onto the bank, still pecking at each other, then pecking for crumbs before retreating to the water.

"They mate for life, you know," Marlon said.

"I wish I were dead," Sonny said.

"You would be if it weren't for my clumsy efforts," Marlon said.

"Marlon, quit putting yourself down," Sonny said.

"You're right," Marlon said. "Why waste time talking about a piece of shit like me?" And then he glanced around surreptitiously to see if they were being watched. An attendant was heading across the lawn to the Administration Building, but they were hidden from his view by the foliage. The Japanese gardener was on his hands and knees, his back to them, completely involved in his work.

"I've got something for you," Marlon said then.

"For me?"

Marlon shook his head and proudly reached behind his back, under his robe, and pulled out a length of rope—good, heavy rope, with a noose tied at one end.

"A way out," Marlon said.

"Hanging?" Sonny said. It was way down on his list. A last resort, the end. He had no idea why, but the idea of hanging frightened him almost as much as the thought of living.

Marlon had taken his arm and walked him a few yards to a tree near the fence that was blocked from the gardener's view. The tree had a branch about seven feet off the ground. Marlon had shinnied a short way up the trunk and was looping one end of the rope around the limb. Sonny watched him apprehensively, but he did not attempt to stop Marlon.

"Hanging," Marlon said, drawing the word out as if it were a delicacy. "It's simple. It's quiet. It's cheap. There's a reason these things become a tradition."

"I wonder if it hurts," Sonny said. He had a terrible feeling that it would hurt.

Marlon stopped his efforts and looked at Sonny quizzically. "Are you changing your mind again?"

"No . . . no," Sonny said hastily. "It's just that. . . . Well, Dr. Maneet was so well adjusted right up to the minute he croaked. Why can't I be like that?"

"I understand he had a disease much less painful than yours," Marlon said.

"True," Sonny said.

"He also had four children and a wife of thirty-five years."

Sonny nodded. "I suspected that," he said.

"You have no family life," Marlon continued.

"True," Sonny said.

"He did meaningful work, enriching his own life and

helping others. You sell lakeside lots where there's no lake."

"Thanks for the pep talk, Marlon."

"You're welcome," Marlon said, catching the loose end of the rope and securing it around the branch. He held the noose out invitingly and crooked his fingers at Sonny; and as if drawn by a magnet, Sonny walked to the tree and stood under the rope.

The rope was too short, or the branch was too high. But it didn't matter. What mattered was that Sonny could not get the noose around his neck.

"Wait," Marlon said, sliding to the ground. "You can climb on my shoulders." Marlon bent over and presented his back to Sonny, who took a deep breath and willed himself to stop thinking. Marlon had positioned himself directly beneath the noose.

Sonny put a knee on Marlon's back. Marlon had braced himself with his elbows. Sonny was sure he must be in pain because of his broken wrist, but Marlon didn't even make a sound as Sonny transferred his weight to Marlon's back. The noose was in reach.

"How are we going to do this?" Sonny asked.

"Put it around your neck," Marlon said.

Sonny put the noose around his neck.

"Now what?" Sonny said.

"I just step out from under you."

"Isn't the hangee usually sitting on a horse?"

"A horse? A Polack? What's the difference? You want a horse? You got a horse!" Marlon whinnied, reared back, and galloped out from under Sonny.

There was a terrible wrenching, and a tightness around his throat, and he couldn't breathe, and the rope loosened unexpectedly just enough to let Sonny's toes reach the ground, just barely reach the ground, and he couldn't talk, and he couldn't breathe, and this was awful! Awful! He was being strangled slowly instead of being hanged, and it was going to take forever, and he couldn't stand it! He couldn't stand it! There was nothing he could do. *Do something,* he yelled silently, unable to utter the words.

And then he sensed rather than saw Marlon scrambling back up the tree, and the rope was tugged and loosened, and tugged again, and Sonny was grabbing at the rope and pulling, trying to get a hold on the tree trunk, anything to keep from prolonging this limbo filled with pain.

"Sonny, you're resisting again" Marlon said, his voice revealing his agitation.

Sonny managed a sound that resembled a croak.

"Yes, you are!" Marlon complained.

And then there was a single tremendous yank on the rope, and it snapped somewhere up above the noose and Sonny fell to the ground, his neck sore, air flooding back into his lungs, and he was furious, outraged, angrier than he had ever been in his life, and he tore the noose from his neck and grabbed Marlon's ankle and pulled him from the tree, throwing him to the ground.

"Why did you stop!" he yelled, his hands on the flesh of Marlon's neck. "I told you not to stop! You almost had me! Next time don't stop, no matter what I say or do . . . understand?" He tightened his grip and banged Marlon's head against the ground, fighting off Marlon's hands.

"Do you understand?" he said, choking harder. "Don't stop killing me no matter what I say!"

And then Sonny realized that Marlon was making desperate noises in his throat, and that his face had begun to turn blue, and he removed his hands from Marlon's throat, looking at them as if they were things apart, no part of himself.

Marlon sat up and gingerly felt his throat, watching Sonny, a peculiar look of triumph on his face. Does the triumph also belong to the victim? Sonny suddenly wondered. It was an incongruous thought, had no place in his present scheme of things; and he looked at his hands again, differently, wondering how Marlon had felt when his hands had clutched his father's neck. . . .

The sound of a truck backfiring cracked through the afternoon. The gardener had started the engine and was now reloading his sacks and equipment on the back of his open-bed truck.

"Well, will you look at that?" Sonny said. "Do you see what I see?"

But Marlon was engrossed in his own thoughts, silently watching Sonny and stroking his neck. The wrist that was in the cast lay on his lap clutching the rope, which still had some length, the noose still tied at one end. Marlon's legs were stretched out before him. A slipper had come off in the fray. He was looking inward, his eyes wide and round and blank.

"Marlon!" Sonny said sharply, and the man came back from his reverie, moving almost immediately to get on his knees and then to scramble to his feet, brushing at the dirt on his gown. Now he, too, was looking at the truck.

"That's my escape," Sonny said. "I think I can escape in that gardener's truck."

"The back entrance," Marlon said. "He goes in and out the back entrance. The gate will be open."

And then the gardener tossed his work overalls in the back of the truck and was returning to the fence to pick up his final sack, and Sonny was running across the lawn, running as fast as he could, running for the plate on his only home run, an inside-the-parker, and he was behind the wheel, and gunning the engine, and pulling the door closed behind him, and the truck lurched because he had forgotten to release the emergency brake, and then he was off, off across the grass, and the gardener was running from the fence, way too late, and way too puny, and Sonny glanced around but Marlon was nowhere to be seen—God, that man was like a shadow!—and the gate was there, and it was open, and Sonny slowed down and turned into the street, leaning back against the seat of the truck, forcing himself to relax, driving slowly, obeying all the rules.

Chapter Nine

"HELLO, MARY ELLEN."

Mary Ellen, shocked by the sound of Sonny's voice, his presence in her kitchen, dropped the glass she was holding. Red wine spilled on the floor, but the glass didn't break.

"Sonny! What are you doing here?"

Sonny remained in the doorway, watching her. She was dressed in white, a soft white blouse and a pleated skirt, and she looked very young and very sweet. She always looked young and sweet. The sink was filled with dirty dishes, and the disorder was worse than he remembered. Mary Ellen's disorder was always worse than he remembered. And why was she dressed, anyway? She usually lounged around the place in a robe or jeans.

"Answer me, Sonny," Mary Ellen said. "You look so strange! What are you doing here?"

"I got a better question. Where are you going all dressed up?"

"To visit you in the hospital," Mary Ellen said.

Sonny started to snap at her, but controlled himself and went looking for a sponge to sop up the wine. Mary Ellen hadn't made a move in that direction.

"Why aren't you there?" Mary Ellen said, walking to the sink and producing some paper towels. "I mean, what are you doing here?" she asked again.

"I thought it'd be easier if I visited you. You know how lousy your car runs."

And then it hit—the pain in his stomach—he had missed his medication; it was a seven . . . oh, God, it was bad! He squatted on his heels and bent his head between his knees, and Mary Ellen was patting him on the back, trying to get him to stand up, and somehow they were back in the living room and she had helped him to lie on the bed. He tried to raise himself up on his elbow, but the movement made him dizzy. He was feeling feverish. He had forgotten how bad it really was.

"Oh, baby," Mary Ellen said, lying down and cradling him in her arms. "Can I get you something?"

The pain began to ease then, and Sonny stretched out his legs. "Do you have any milk, Mary Ellen?"

"No." Her eyes were sad, like a calf's.

"Anything cold, then. Coke, orange juice, apple juice . . . ?"

"Damn," she said. "I don't have any of those. Can I get you something else?"

"Mary Ellen, there *isn't* anything else!"

Unexpectedly he began to cough, a deep, wracking cough that propelled him into a sitting position. Instantly Mary Ellen was off the bed, heading for the kitchen, and Sonny heard the water running in the sink. It was bad, very bad. It reminded him of the old man in the hospital's terminal ward. *He* had been coughing like this, deep, wracking coughs. Sonny's chest hurt with the effort, and then Mary Ellen returned and was pounding him two, three, four times on the back and then handing him the glass of water, stroking his hair as he gulped it down.

"Honey, if you're going to use jelly glasses, you should wipe out the jelly before. . . ." Were those really tears forming in her eyes? "Aw, forget it, sweets," he said, pulling her to him and hugging her close. She felt so good, smelled so good. . . .

"Sonny, you should be in the hospital, shouldn't you?" she said.

"No, no," he said vehemently. "No more other people telling me what to do with my life . . . or death."

He released her then and headed for the dresser, pulling open the drawers.

"What are you doing?" Mary Ellen said.

"Looking for my clothes."

Mary Ellen crossed to the corner beyond the bed, pushed the tabby cat away, and rummaged through a pile. "Here are your clothes," she said. "I ironed them. You've got some sneakers in the closet."

But Sonny was still rummaging in the dresser.

"Come on, Mary Ellen," he said then, a rough edge to his voice. "You know what I'm looking for. Where is it?"

"I hid it," she said, her eyes darting toward the bathroom.

That's what I like about her, Sonny thought. She's so good at keeping secrets.

"No, Sonny, no!" Mary Ellen shrieked as he headed for the bathroom. He tossed off her attempt to stop him, knocking over the apartment's only plant in the process, an event that sent the tabby cat yowling out of his way. Sonny threaded his way through the kitchen to the bathroom, attacking the cabinet under the sink and the medicine chest, turning over the hamper and kicking through the dirty clothes, flinging open the shower curtain, and there, hidden in the vent, its dark color visible in the slots, was the gun.

"You found it," Mary Ellen said dully when he returned to the living room hefting the .38 automatic.

"Yup. In the shower. Behind the vent."

"How'd you find it?"

"Finding the gun was easy," Sonny said. "Finding the shower was tough."

"I'm calling the police," Mary Ellen said.

Sonny's hand raised itself automatically. "One move and I'll shoot," he said, but Mary Ellen gave him a glance and no more than that, ignoring the gun, and continued heading for the phone.

"Not you, Mary Ellen," he said. "Myself." She stopped then, afraid, and Sonny carefully lifted the gun and held it to his temple. The muzzle was cold. He wondered if the gun was functional. What would steam from the shower do to it?

"That's right, baby," he said quickly when Mary hesitated. "Stop right there. Touch that phone and I'll splatter my brains all over your walls. Not that anyone would notice."

"Sonny, you are driving me crazy!" Mary Ellen shrieked.

"That's all right," he said, keeping the gun to his temple and using his left hand to begin unbuttoning his pajamas. "You won't have to put up with me much longer."

Mary Ellen came and helped him take the pajama top off and put on his shirt, and then she was against his chest, and he lowered the gun and held her.

"Oh, Sonny, I feel so awful. Sometimes I think if I could have loved you more . . . maybe . . . maybe you wouldn't be dying." She drew back into the circle of his arms and looked at him, running the back of her hand along his beard. "I . . . maybe I caused it," she blurted out then, biting her lower lip.

"Don't be silly. You can't give somebody a blood disease. It's a gift from God."

"But if I would have been more what you wanted . . . given in more . . . something!"

"No, honey . . . no. There's nothing you could have done to—" And then a crazy thought ran through Sonny's head, a dreadful thought. "Maybe . . . just maybe . . . if you would have come at least once. . . ."

Mary Ellen let out an anguished moan and buried her head against his chest, making no attempt to stop the sudden sobs that wracked her body.

"Oh, no, no, don't. Stop, Mary Ellen. I'm sorry.

Don't blame yourself. Come on, girl. That was mean of me. You know . . . with all my whining and moaning, I think I had more fun in this relationship than you did."

Mary Ellen shook her head against his chest, refusing to look up at him.

"Yes, yes, yes, I did," Sonny said. "And maybe the reason I loved you is *because* I couldn't have you completely. You have to admit that sounds like me."

Sonny released her then, sitting her firmly on the edge of the bed, placing the gun on the bookcase behind him where she could not get at it without having to fight him. Quickly he removed the rest of the hospital clothing and finished dressing. He took a few seconds to look at his reflection in the mirror near the closet—yes, he did like the way the beard looked—and then sat on the bed next to Mary Ellen and turned her around so that she was lying in his arms, her body across his lap.

"Look, baby," he said, stroking her, wiping the tears from her face, "with all the shit I've given you, you must know that I was *always* turned on by you. That's worth a lot, darling."

Mary Ellen was getting herself under control, and she nodded silently, sniffing.

"I just wish you'd try to understand what I'm doing now . . . this suicide," Sonny said, pronouncing the word clearly and without emphasis. It felt like a triumph.

"I think I'm starting to, Sonny," Mary Ellen said in a little voice. "I do. I've been selfish, trying to keep you here a little longer." And then she put her head down on his thigh and whispered, "You do what you have to do."

"You mean it's okay with you for me to commit suicide?" There, he'd said it again to her.

Mary Ellen's hand was playing with the buttons on his shirt. Now she lifted her head a bit and looked at him with her big blue eyes. "Yes," she said, and then sobbed again and turned her face away.

"Baby!" Sonny said. He kissed her, a long kiss, a tender kiss, a kiss of great feeling; and then his mouth got hard, almost brutal, and he had her by the shoulders and was pushing her away and holding her at the same time.

"You could never let me kill myself if you *really* loved me," he said.

"Sonny!" Mary Ellen screamed, breaking away from him. "You're crazy! I can't please you! Stop picking on me!"

Sonny started to say something to her, but what was there to say? She was right. He was crazy, and he was picking on her. Why? He didn't know why. Why did apples ripen in the fall? Why didn't he ever place higher than third in the diving competitions? Why did that shadow figure that walked in front of the windows outside remind him of Marlon Borunki?

He retrieved the gun and gave Mary Ellen a peck of a kiss on the tip of her nose. What a lovely nose.

"I'm sorry, honey. 'Bye," he said, and headed for the door.

"Sonny, don't go. Don't go yet!" Mary Ellen commanded.

"I have to. Let go of my arm. I'm just going to go off somewhere and swallow lead."

"But . . . but . . . there's something important I have to tell you."

"What? That you fucked some other guy? That he made you come until you screamed for mercy? Who cares about stuff like that now? I've got a date with a thirty-eight." He grabbed her arms above the elbows and shook her. "Who was it? That guy with the Honda? Someone I've never even seen? The oven-door repairman? Is that why it isn't fixed yet?"

"No, no, nothing like that," she said, and Sonny released her arms because fear had come into her magnificent blue eyes, and she was a child and children shouldn't be made to be afraid. "It's just that . . . the gun isn't loaded, Sonny."

"What?"

"I took the bullets out right after you gave it to me, and threw them away. I was afraid someone might hurt themselves."

"That was very stupid!" Sonny said, examining the gun, pulling off the safety, and out of frustration pointing it at the wall and pulling the trigger.

The shot missed the tabby cat with inches to spare, and Sonny let out a shriek of pain as the cat jumped a good three feet in the air and came down to sink its claws into his thigh.

Mary Ellen was shaking. She reached out a hand to Sonny's arm to steady herself, but he shook her off.

"Everything you do is half-assed!" he said.

"I thought I unloaded all the bullets," Mary Ellen said.

" 'I thought I unloaded all the bullets,' " Sonny mimicked, throwing the gun as hard as he could at the window near the front door. It crashed through, breaking the glass.

"Get out! Get out!" Mary Ellen was screaming.

"I'm glad I didn't kill myself here," Sonny said, kicking a can of catfood across the floor. "It would have taken them days to find my body."

"Get out!"

"You bet," Sonny said, heading for the door. "I've got a date with a bullet salesman."

But the gun wasn't there. Not in the bushes under Mary Ellen's window, although he cut a finger on some broken glass, not on the curb or under the truck, either. He checked the bushes next door, also, and under the cars in front of and behind the truck. His eye was drawn to the back of the flatbed. The gardener's overalls were gone, and Marlon's rope was lying near the sacks of manure that piled up almost to the rear window. Could he be . . . ? No, he couldn't be.

Sonny shook his head and searched the area again. The gun was gone. A neighborhood kid? He looked up. Mary Ellen was standing at the window watching him, crying profusely, one hand at her throat, her beautiful face contorted with grief and unhappiness. Something inside Sonny melted, and with a last fruitless glance he headed back into Mary Ellen's apartment, heading straight for Tabby.

He picked up the cat and gave it a pet, then threw it down hard. "I forgot to say good-bye to the cats," he said, having no more luck finding the kitten than he had had finding the gun.

"And as long as I'm here. . . ." He opened his arms to her, and Mary Ellen ran across the room, embracing him.

"I loved you, Mary Ellen," he said.

And perhaps because he left without making love to her, Sonny headed for the ocean, the need for solitude strongly on him. It wasn't simply being alone that he wanted—there was plenty of that at La Playa—it was the *solitude,* the sense of being able to control a piece of space, and the sound of the water, the look of a beach.

He wished he had asked Mary Ellen for some money, and began to punish himself with thoughts of food— spareribs from the place down the block from his office, his mother's pot roast, Julie's brownies. . . . On an impulse he opened the glove compartment. He laughed out loud. Right on top of a wicked-looking pruning knife, attached to a shopping list printed in Japanese, was a ten-dollar bill. He made a detour for a shopping center a few blocks away. There was an ice cream place there that made the best snacks in town. Vanilla, he wanted. With chocolate ice cream.

He dawdled in the ice cream place, taking his time, and ordered a second shake, a coffee one, to take with him, holding the container between his legs as he headed for the Coast Highway, driving carefully, his speed steady, a sense of finality once again beginning to propel him, a sense of inevitability, of rightness.

He was heading for the dead-end street where Marty had a friend who sometimes let them use his house. It was a secluded place, and the afternoon had turned windy. The surf was high, and the beach would be deserted.

Why hadn't he made love to Mary Ellen? he wondered. Was he afraid that the feelings would make him want to serve out his time?

A car shot past in the passing lane, and Sonny had a glimpse of a young girl who reminded him of Julie. She was looking at something in the back of the truck. Sonny glanced in the rearview mirror but saw nothing except the top of an evergreen shrub.

Consciously he pushed the thought of Julie away from him, concentrating on the road, watching the ocean spray itself against formations of rocks. God, it was beautiful. And violent. And as unpredictable as the swans. It was rough today.

The first time Marty had taken him to the beach house he had also brought along a brunette with blonde pubic hair. The first and last of her species that Sonny had ever met. Loretta, her name was, and she had done it with both of them, him and Marty, and they had gone at it all night.

Sonny finished the coffee milk shake and tossed the container on the truck's floor, shifting for a difficult climbing curve. He wished he were driving the Jaguar. He loved this road in the Jaguar.

But he was feeling exhilarated nevertheless, watching the odometer spit out the miles, and then he was there, pulling down the dead-end street, parking at the end, near an outcropping of rocks. He put the change from the ten-dollar bill in the glove compartment, weighing down the bills with the pruning knife, and left the keys in the ignition slot.

He could feel the pounding of the surf on his skin. The smell made his nostrils quiver. He kicked off his sneakers one by one, and sent them sailing as far as he could throw in different directions.

It was hard to look directly at the water, and Sonny stopped to pick up several shells, one a nearly perfect conch, then he looked around and collected more, piling them in a mound in the center of a circle he made with his belt. But it proved a task too slow to satisfy him, and he filled in the mound with sand, sticking the conch, point down, into the top. It was a nice piece of handiwork. He backed away from it to take a look from a different perspective, the surf lapping at his heels. He started to remove his pants, but thought better of it and rolled up the cuffs instead.

The surf was trying to keep him from backing away to look at the mound. It pushed at his heels and the backs of his legs, threatening to knock him off his feet. So he played a trick with it, unexpectedly walking backward until he was in the water to his waist, and then he dove backward to release his feet from the command of the sand, and at once he got dunked, water filling his nostrils, water blinding him.

And he turned then and swam hard, as if he had dived into a saltwater pond and was heading for the edge.

But it had never been like this, not so rough, with swells that already blocked his view of the shore when once he turned to look, and it was so dark, so very dark, pools were never that dark.

He had a sudden crazy impulse to sing, and he knew Dr. Maneet had been wrong—this was the way for him, it had to be the way for him, because there was no way he could get back. There was no way he could get back! He was too far out!

And the ocean was reaching up for him then like a hungry mouth, a cold, hungry mouth that wanted to devour him, to swallow him alive. . . .

And he wasn't going to make it! The pain in his stomach! There was no sense in struggle, he was being bounced about, no will of his own—a breath! He got to fill his lungs. Once. Twice. He was closer to shore now! If he could only move his arms.

He didn't want to die! He wanted to live. Of course he wanted to live!

He was being scraped along the churning bottom of the sea, pushed towards the shore, rolling over and getting cut, hurt; he knew he was being hurt, but he was too afraid, too out of control, to feel it. He had the crazy notion that if he could stand up, just get on his feet, everything would be all right. All he had to do was put out a hand and stop himself and then stand up, that's all he had to do—just put out a hand and stop himself and stand up. He was going to have to breathe in, his body would be denied no longer, and he put out a hand and stopped himself from rolling over, but he didn't have the strength to stand, just enough strength to get on his knees.

Miraculously, he was on the beach.

He opened his mouth and gasped in the air, his body shuddering to forget its agony, flopping over on his back, exhausted, too exhausted to move, too tired to move.

Another involuntary shudder wracked his body, and he sat up to vomit out some seawater, opening up his eyes.

Marlon stood there, holding the gun. It was held loosely in the hand with the broken wrist. The weight of it must have hurt. He was wearing the Japanese gardener's overalls, which came halfway to his calves and did not button at either side. There was on his face a look of detached determination.

"Wait!" Sonny managed to say.

Marlon shook his head and slowly raised the gun to aim it at Sonny's head. Sonny responded automatically, doing the only thing he was capable of doing, picking up and throwing a handful of sand in Marlon's face. Marlon staggered and wiped at his eyes, but Sonny couldn't follow through, he couldn't get to Marlon, and then Marlon was aiming again and Sonny shut his eyes and waited.

He opened his eyes.

Marlon was staring at the gun, the cylinder open.

"It's empty," Marlon said, bewilderment on his face. "But I heard you test-fire it!"

"It was the only bullet," Sonny said. He hadn't even heard the gun click. The sound had been lost in the noise of the sea.

"I can't do anything right." Marlon sat down on the sand next to Sonny and pouted, sticking out his upper lip.

"Stop that, Marlon," Sonny said. "I'm glad. I've changed my mind. I want to live . . . for a little while, anyway. That doctor was right, Marlon. The reason I keep failing is because I don't want to die. So I'm taking back everything I said, and you have to promise to quit trying to kill me."

"But your pain," Marlon said. "You've been like this every time. You made me promise to help you end your fears."

"And now I'm asking you to take it back."

"I don't think it's in your best interests," Marlon said.

"I don't care what you think!" Sonny said, taking the gun from Marlon's hand and pointing it at him.

"It's empty," Marlon said. "And I don't think you like me anymore."

"Yes, I do," Sonny said. "Now promise."

Marlon looked at him, then looked away, rubbing his cheeks, then looking back.

"Okay," he said. "I promise."

Sonny felt the smile starting at his toes, and, getting on his knees, he drew back his arm and pitched a strike

170

with the gun, hitting a patch of white water at the top of a breaking wave.

He got up and tested his legs. They were weak, his knees rubbery, but they held him up. He had lost both socks. He began walking toward the truck. The sand felt terrific.

"I love you, Sonny." Marlon's voice was nearly drowned out by the breaking of a wave, yet there was something peculiar about it, something which made the hackles on Sonny's neck rise. Slowly he turned. Marlon was standing maybe twenty feet away. The gardener's pruning knife was in his left hand, point up, and he was beginning to walk toward Sonny, his lips drawn back, an expression on his face Sonny had never seen before.

Somewhere, from deep inside, Sonny found the strength to run. He ran, heading for the truck, for the road, for people, praying that his muscles wouldn't cramp, that he wouldn't fall, because if he did, there was doubt about it. It would be the end. The end.

THE BIG BESTSELLERS
ARE AVON BOOKS

☐	Lancelot Walker Percy	36582	$2.25
☐	Oliver's Story Erich Segal	36343	$1.95
☐	Snowblind Robert Sabbag	36947	$1.95
☐	A Capitol Crime Lawrence Meyer	37150	$1.95
☐	Voyage Sterling Hayden	37200	$2.50
☐	Lady Oracle Margaret Atwood	35444	$1.95
☐	Humboldt's Gift Saul Bellow	38810	$2.25
☐	Mindbridge Joe Haldeman	33605	$1.95
☐	Polonaise Piers Paul Read	33894	$1.95
☐	A Fringe of Leaves Patrick White	36160	$1.95
☐	Founder's Praise Joanne Greenberg	34702	$1.95
☐	To Jerusalem and Back Saul Bellow	33472	$1.95
☐	A Sea-Change Lois Gould	33704	$1.95
☐	The Moon Lamp Mark Smith	32698	$1.75
☐	The Surface of Earth Reynolds Price	29306	$1.95
☐	The Monkey Wrench Gang Edward Abbey	30114	$1.95
☐	Beyond the Bedroom Wall Larry Woiwode	29454	$1.95
☐	Jonathan Livingston Seagull Richard Bach	34777	$1.75
☐	Working Studs Terkel	34660	$2.50
☐	Shardik Richard Adams	27359	$1.95
☐	Anya Susan Fromberg Schaeffer	25262	$1.95
☐	The Bermuda Triangle Charles Berlitz	25254	$1.95
☐	Watership Down Richard Adams	19810	$2.25

Available at better bookstores everywhere, or order direct from the publisher.

AVON BOOKS, Mail Order Dept., 250 West 55th St., New York, N.Y. 10019

Please send me the books checked above. I enclose $_____(please include 25¢ per copy for postage and handling). Please use check or money order—sorry, no cash or COD's. Allow 4-6 weeks for delivery.

Mr/Mrs/Miss_____

Address_____

City_____State/Zip_____

BB 5-78

SNOW BLIND

ROBERT SABBAG

A BRIEF CAREER
IN THE COCAINE TRADE

From Amagansett to Bogotá, from straight to
scam to snafu then the slam, SNOWBLIND is
an all-out, nonstop, mind-jolting journey through
the chic and violent world of Zachary Swan, the
real-life Madison Avenue executive who em-
barked on a fabulous, shortlived career in smug-
gling——bringing better living through chemistry
from South American soil to New York nose.

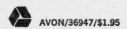

AVON/36947/$1.95

SNOW 3-78

AVON ◆ THE BEST IN
BESTSELLING ENTERTAINMENT

☐ **Your Erroneous Zones**		
Dr. Wayne W. Dyer	33373	$2.25
☐ **Majesty** Robert Lacey	36327	$2.25
☐ **Q&A** Edwin Torres	36590	$1.95
☐ **If the Reaper Ride** Elizabeth Norman	37135	$1.95
☐ **This Other Eden** Marilyn Harris	36301	$2.25
☐ **Berlin Tunnel 21** Donald Lindquist	36335	$2.25
☐ **Ghost Fox** James Houston	35733	$1.95
☐ **Ambassador** Stephen Longstreet	31997	$1.95
☐ **The Boomerang Conspiracy**		
Michael Stanley	35535	$1.95
☐ **Gypsy Lady** Shirlee Busbee	36145	$1.95
☐ **Good Evening Everybody**		
Lowell Thomas	35105	$2.25
☐ **Jay J. Armes, Investigator**		
Jay J. Armes and Frederick Nolan	36494	$1.95
☐ **The Mists of Manitoo**		
Lois Swann	33613	$1.95
☐ **Flynn** Gregory Mcdonald	34975	$1.95
☐ **Lovefire** Julia Grice	34538	$1.95
☐ **Hollywood Is a Four Letter Town**		
James Bacon	33399	$1.95
☐ **The Search for Joseph Tully**		
William H. Hallahan	33712	$1.95
☐ **Delta Blood** Barbara Ferry Johnson	32664	$1.95
☐ **Wicked Loving Lies** Rosemary Rogers	30221	$1.95
☐ **Moonstruck Madness** Laurie McBain	31385	$1.95
☐ **ALIVE: The Story of the Andes Survivors**		
Piers Paul Read	39164	$2.25
☐ **Sweet Savage Love** Rosemary Rogers	38869	$2.25
☐ **The Flame and the Flower**		
Kathleen E. Woodiwiss	35485	$2.25
☐ **I'm OK—You're OK**		
Thomas A. Harris, M.D.	28282	$2.25

The supercharged novel of the Indy 500—
where the fastest action
isn't on the track!

SPECTATOR SPORT

JAMES
ALEXANDER
THOM

*In the stands, under the stands,
behind motel doors—SPECTATOR SPORT is the blazing
saga of a classic race, where love is fast,
death is sudden, and the only god is speed!*

Pulsing with the reckless passions of the fans,
who plunge into fantastic mud-drenched
orgies, and the high-octane desires of the driv-
ers and their women, who live on the edge—
SPECTATOR SPORT is a novel of overwhelm-
ing human drama and of a man and a woman
in a desperate race for real love.

AVON/37705/$1.95

SPSP 5-78